WHAT'S AN AVERAGE KID LIKE ME DOING WAY UP HERE?

IVY RUCKMAN

A YEARLING BOOK

Published by
Dell Publishing Co., Inc.
1 Dag Hammarskjold Plaza
New York, New York 10017

Yearling ® TM 913705, Dell Publishing Co., Inc.

ISBN: 0-440-49448-6

Reprinted by arrangement with Delacorte Press
Printed in the United States of America

May 1984

10 9 8 7 6 5 4 3 2

CW

For Allan,
who knows the reasons why.

1

Middle is my middle name. Only it's spelled different. I'm Norman Midd*al* Gates, after my grandfather. I go to Fortuna Middle School, sit in the middle of the room, answer "here" somewhere in the middle of roll call, and am always *mid*way through lunch when the cafeteria bell rings.

If I also parted my hair you-know-where, you wouldn't read another page of this book. But I don't, so I hope you will. Actually, my big sister, Dee, just gave me a permanent ("So Lisa will notice you," she says), but, worrywart that I am, I figure it's the guys that will be noticing most.

So here I am, Normal Norman, coming to you without so much as a sponsor.

"Herrrre's Norman!" you might say. "A kid who is no threat to substitute teachers . . . who has never been kicked out of shop . . . who never once in his life forgot his jockstrap or his orthodontic appointment!"

It's enough to make you gag, isn't it?

Except.

Except for what happened at Fortuna Middle School between February 10 and the middle of May this year.

I had no idea I was going to extinguish—I mean *dis*-tinguish—myself. Who would have predicted my name and face would appear on two TV channels? Who'd have thought an average kid like me could generate enough news to fill one whole page of the newspaper?

Maybe my father suspected. Maybe that's why he up and left about the time it all began. They say dogs start barking before an earthquake. Maybe some subterranean rumble reached him before it did me and that's why he took off. I'll wonder about that until the day I die . . . or until I see him again.

2

ex tin guish—v.t., to put out, put an end to; to
        eclipse, as by superior brilliance

dis tin guish—v.t., to mark off as different; to make
        prominent

Monday's vocabulary words, printed in black Magic Marker, were stuck to the refrigerator door with strawberry magnets. My mother, Barbara Gates–the-English-teacher, was working on the Noah Principle that second week of February: Pairs were twice as good as singles.

"Why do you confuse those two words?" Mom said, looking at me. She was warming up for her first-period class at Driggs Memorial High School. She always warmed up on Dee and me while we were getting into our yogurt and granola.

"*Ex* means 'out,' 'out of,' or 'former,' " she went on, pouring a cup of coffee for herself.

"Like ex-husband?" I said. I couldn't get used to setting only three places at the breakfast table.

"Right, good example. Though I hope you're not including your father in that category, Norman. Michael is *absent*—"

"*Ab* meaning 'away' or 'away from,'" my sister, Dee, butted in, mimicking Mom.

"—but he's not *ex!*" Mom thumped my sister on the head as she passed with her coffee cup.

I sighed. *Ex* or *ab*, it amounted to the same thing. I wondered how long Mom would keep up the pretense that Dad had simply taken a sabbatical to climb mountains.

"How's *ex*cavate for an example?" Dee said, tossing her straight blond hair over her shoulder. "That's what you need to do in your room, *Normie*."

Being a know-it-all teen-ager, my sister, Delilah, never misses a chance to dig. I stuck my tongue out at her, making sure it was covered with yogurt. She looked away in a hurry.

I should tell you right here, my sister's the most fas-tid-i-ous (Friday's word) person I ever met! She washes her hair every day, won't wear clothes unless they're clean, brushes the enamel right off her teeth. If Lisa Harrington is half as fas-tid-i-ous as my dumb sister, I may never ask for her hand in marriage. (I thought of Lisa's hand as she held the pickled frog in science class, her arm straight out in front, her face turning green like the frog.) I'd have to do some heavy thinking about Lisa's fastidiousness. You can't be too careful when it comes to choosing a person of the opposite sex.

"Look at the time, Mom!" Dee was bouncing up and down on her chair. "You're going to be late again."

I sometimes wondered *who* was parenting *whom*.

"Oh dear, it's seven twenty, how'd that happen?" Mom was up from the table in a flash, flying around the family room scooping up books, tripping over Animal, blowing

4

kisses as she whizzed by. She stopped at the door to the garage and dived into her purse for keys. "Anybody staying after school tonight?"

"No," we said.

"Hurry, Mom!" Dee was bouncing again.

Mom bolted out of the kitchen. Though she disappeared from sight, she hadn't stopped talking. "Lock up, guys. And leave the radio on for the burglars."

Dee laughed and shook her head like an adult. "Mom's going to be *so* disappointed if we don't get burglarized some day."

I laughed too, just to be sociable. I didn't think what she'd said was funny at all.

Dee stood to pour herself some coffee as soon as Mom started the engine. Besides being fastidious, my sister is a sneak.

"I'll take a cup," I said, not waiting to be asked.

"You will *not!*"

I finished my orange juice.

Five days of the week now, since taking a new teaching job this semester, our mother was making the same identical exit. After all those years shoving us out the door . . . now we were doing the shoving. It made me a little sad. Not that I need to be hugged and kissed anymore. Going on thirteen, who needs mushy good-byes? It's just that the house is so quiet after she leaves.

Anyway, my father had only been gone a week at that time and I was practically a basket case already. As if my new responsibilities as man of the house weren't enough to weigh me down, that very day—February 10—the school board announced its decision about Fortuna Middle School.

5

3

School had droned on and on that Monday, with the sun coming out of the clouds three times by actual count. I should have known something awful was about to happen. For one thing, Lisa Harrington returned a note from me marked "No comment," which made me wonder if I should give up on her. A crushing blow like that should have clued me.

Then, too, as the day wore on, Steve Pugsley's feet began to stink. They always juiced up during gym class, then turned smelly while he sat there beside me during unified math.

The last straw was Mr. Henry's assigning two pages of story problems at the end of the period. I felt terrible. I couldn't see one reason why I shouldn't go into an all-time rock-bottom slump.

About then, however, the PA crackled to life.

"Your attention, please!"

It was Mr. Clayton himself, the Big C. Now, *his* voice can always get our adrenaline flowing. Our principal is the kind who never gets on the PA unless the situation is serious. Snowballing, locker-jamming, water bombs—all that stuff is left to the vice. But when Principal Clayton speaks, Fortuna listens!

6

"Teachers . . . students . . . our family at Fortuna . . ."

For a minute there I thought he was praying. A reverent hush fell over the room.

"Fortuna Middle School, which has meant so much to all of us"—he paused and I could hear him swallow—"is going to be closed at the end of May. Forever."

Steve sat straight up in his desk for the first time, grinning. Everyone looked at everyone else. Mr. Henry turned pale, I swear it! I stared at the back of Lisa's head, two rows in front of me, wishing she'd turn around.

"Please go quietly to the auditorium instead of your sixth-period class," Mr. Clayton continued. "All afterschool activities will be canceled today. Go directly to the auditorium when the bell rings."

It was over. That fast. February 10 marked the beginning of the end and we all knew it.

"Are you going to open your envelope?" Steve asked me after school once we got a safe distance from Fortuna.

"Clayton said not to. Look, it says 'For the Parents.' Can't you read?"

"Who cares what it says? I'm opening mine."

That's the kind of guy Steve is. My mom says he's straight out of the Old West's lawless tradition. If anyone ever needed hanging, Steve would be right there with a rope.

Steve sat down on the curb in front of Bogucki's Bakery, in a place where the snow had melted. I watched him rip open the envelope we were supposed to take home sealed. It was already black around the edges from his dirty hands.

"Oh well," I sighed, and made him move over. There were advantages to being Steve's friend.

The letter was long and boring, with a Declining School

7

Enrollment Chart and a graph entitled "School Operating Costs." The part about a bond issue we skipped. It was the busing map on page three that made Steve leap up like he'd been goosed.

"Spit on it, Gates! Look at this!" His eyes were shooting sparks. "They can't do this to us. We been together since kindygarten."

My stomach flopped. I grabbed the letter away from him. Fortuna students, it said, would be bused to *two different schools*. The boundary line divided our neighborhood smack down the middle. Steve and (oh lord, no!) Lisa Harrington would be bused to Clearfield. All the pathetic kids on my street would be sent to Roy Middle School, which is in the other direction.

Not even the smell of hot cinnamon rolls coming out of Bogucki's could console me now. We were doomed, Lisa and I. The truth struck me with all the misery of a twenty-four-hour flu. *Lisa, my love, we are doomed!*

"What about Hansen and Krepps?" Steve threw himself bodily into the snow. "They'll be split up like us!"

They were our star forward and the only six-foot center in the history of middle school basketball. Steve moaned and rolled over, facedown in what was left of Saturday's snowstorm. I couldn't stand to see him like that, so I gave him a kick in the ribs.

"Come on, Pugsley, I'll buy us a chocolate éclair."

"Who can eat?"

I knew how hard he was taking it when he said that.

Three girls came out of the bakery with doughnuts, licking the frosting off their fingers. Little did they know what was in their envelopes! One of them made a face at Steve, who

8

was stretched out like he'd OD'd, then pinched the tip of her nose. I hate girls when they do things like that. The wind wasn't even in the right direction for her to smell anything.

"Maybe it won't happen," I said, rolling Steve over. "Come on, we'll think of something, I promise. We always do."

He got up then and wiped his face on the sleeve of his Levi's jacket. I couldn't believe what I saw, but Steve Pugsley had tears on his cheeks. Fortuna's unofficial heavyweight champ, who averaged one fight a week to keep his title, had *tear streaks* on his face. Why, he hadn't flinched even when our home ec teacher caught him running pins through his calluses and whacked him with her ruler!

It would take two éclairs apiece to get us feeling better, I decided as we walked into the bakery.

Then I had a terrible thought. What would happen to Bogucki's when Fortuna closed? Or the 7-Eleven at the bottom of the hill? Or even Slim's Gas and Go! That's where we filled our bike tires on the way to school and bought our licorice supply. Fortuna *had* to stay open!

"Four éclairs and a dozen doughnut holes," I told Mrs. Minschell, the baker's wife.

Steve smiled bravely as I blew my week's allowance. "Let's go to your house," he said.

We didn't say much the rest of the way home for eating and thinking. I forced myself to go over each crisis separately at first. When I took on the sum total of all the catastrophes, I considered having a breakdown right there in the middle of the sidewalk. Why did everything have to happen at once? My mom going to work, my dad taking off supposedly climbing mountains, and now my school closing, just like that! As if a guy doesn't have enough problems with puberty and math! I needed help.

"If my dad was here, he'd know what to do about Fortuna," I blurted out, breaking the silence between Steve and me.

"But he ain't," Steve snapped back. "He's nowhere near here. You got to get used to it, man, he's *gone*."

"Tell me about it!" I said sarcastically, kicking a clump of snow off the sidewalk.

"I'm telling you. You gotta stand on your own two feet. My old man went off the same way, remember? 'I'll come back and see you all the time,' he told me, 'we'll go fishing and take trips and all that.' Crap! I can't even remember what he looked like!"

Steve reached in the bag and brought out the last of the doughnut holes. We divided them up and kept on walking toward my house.

Steve said, "I suppose he told you he loved you and all that garbage just before he left . . ."

I didn't answer, but Steve was guessing right.

"They think they're letting you down easy, that's what they think."

I listened to Steve. He was not only six months older and more experienced, he was also sixteen pounds heavier than I was. Five years ago his dad had gone to Mexico, too. That was when his parents got divorced. Steve had never seen him again.

"It's those margaritas they drink down there." Steve started laughing. "They kind of make you go crazy."

I smiled at his drunken staggers and crossed eyes as he tried to make it up my front steps. I guess that's what I like about Steve, when it comes right down to it. He can never be serious for long.

We headed straight for the kitchen then, both of us thirsty after all that bakery stuff. I took out the milk bottle and poured us a couple of tall ones.

We raised our glasses and clinked.

"Here's to Fortuna," I said.

"Fortuna forever!" he added in this serious voice, toasting the school he'd been threatening to vandalize for the last eight years.

Suddenly, the second meaning of *extinguish* shone forth from that refrigerator door like a lighted torch: "To eclipse, as by superior brilliance."

I don't know what happened, but in that moment I was through with being ordinary. *Someone* had to save Fortuna Middle School. Picture a medieval trumpeter standing on the parapet of a castle. Hear that fanfare of brittle-bright notes? That's just the way it was with me. The challenge skittered right up my spine. Someone had to uphold the traditions . . . keep us together . . . Hansen and Krepps, Steve, Lisa and me . . . we were like a family, for crying out loud!

"Don't worry, Pugs." I looked him straight in the eye, which isn't easy when someone's a head taller than you. "Fortuna won't go down without a fight!"

Steve's face brightened at once. He understood fighting better than anything else.

4

"What are we going to do?" I started right in on Mom as soon as she got home from school. "Nobody wants to be bused. It's stupid! Steve going to one place, me another. And what about Fortuna? Our school has this really terrific reputation. They can't do this to us!"

Mom had worked off her shoes and kicked them under the dining room table where she was sitting. She frowned as she read the letter again.

"Can't the parents vote on it or something?" I said. "We living in a dictatorship or what?"

"Makes you wonder sometimes . . ." She was studying the busing map.

"Mom, please, we have to *do* something."

"I know that, Norman, I know that." She padded into the kitchen and poured herself a cup of coffee.

"It's cold," I warned her.

She poured it back, plugged in the pot.

"Get Glenna on the phone," Mom said. "Call her at the cafe. I think we'd better have some neighbors in tonight and talk this over."

Glenna is Steve's mother and she's a waitress part time. If I knew her, she'd arrive about nine with one of those deep-dish apple pies her place is famous for.

Before I could get to the phone, it started ringing. It practically never stopped. Everyone else had the same idea. My mom, who had petitioned for the stop sign four years ago and the streetlight last year, and who'd been room mother since the beginning of time, was the logical person for neighbors to call. They knew they could count on her.

Even through dinner preparations—stirring the Hamburger Delite with one hand, directing me to set the table with the other—Mom kept her end of the conversations going.

"Can Morris come with you tonight?" I heard her ask Edith Sweitzer. "We need to have some men over here. This isn't a feminist issue, you know."

Mom nodded, listening. I could tell Mrs. Sweitzer was making up excuses for Morris.

"Look, Edie, I gotta run. I'm still in my school clothes. Just be here, huh?"

Mom wasn't really still in her school clothes. I don't *think* she teaches barefooted in a slip and sweater.

She dialed another number when Mrs. Sweitzer hung up, inviting someone else to the meeting at our house. Waiting for an answer, she began pointing to the fridge, pantomiming something with her right hand. I couldn't decide if she wanted me to toss a salad or mix up some Kool-Aid. Maybe she was just limbering up her wrist.

I slid off into the family room to watch *M*A*S*H* until she got off the phone. With my mother in charge of Fortuna's future, I felt I could relax a little.

"Norman," she called a minute later. "Come stir the Jell-O before it sets up." I would have already if I'd known what she meant. Mom can be very vague at times.

❈　❈　❈

13

Later, with the living room packed full of neighbors, my mother wasn't vague at all.

"Did anyone know the school board was considering closure of Fortuna?" she asked to start off. Then she wanted to know if anyone had been able to reach Mr. Gray for a comment.

"He probably has his phone off the hook!" Lisa's mother said.

Mr. Gray, I quickly learned, was our area's school board representative. I figured his ears were burning, the way everyone was talking about him.

Actually, the meeting was pretty boring. A few people said they didn't have time to get involved in a "fruitless squabble," as Morris Sweitzer called it. I could tell then that my mother was sorry she'd asked him to come.

When they got around to the nitty-gritties of school financing—and still no one had asked my advice—I decided to go into my parents' bedroom (Mom's room now) and call Lisa on the extension. My sister-the-phone-hog was upstairs studying for a history test with her friend Jennifer, so for once I had the privacy a guy deserves.

I didn't get the shakes until I dialed the last digit. At that point I usually hung up. Well, sometimes I got as far as the first or second ring, and once I even hung on to hear Lisa's musical "Hellooooo." But that night, seeing my mother in action had given me a shot of courage. These were not your normal times!

Jamie, her little brother, answered.

"May I speak to Lisa, please?" I said in this well-modulated voice.

"Who is this?"

"I'm a friend of hers."

"What's your name? Maybe she doesn't want to talk to you."

"Christopher Reeve." *There, rude kid!*

"Leeeeeesa!" he yelled. "Christopher Reeve is on the phone."

My hands started to sweat. She wouldn't believe him, would she?

She didn't believe him, even a little bit.

"Okay, wise guy, what do you want?" she snapped.

"S-sorry about that," I stammered, "but your little brother—"

"Who's speaking, please?"

I admire girls who come right to the point, but all of a sudden I couldn't remember if I was Clark Kent or Superman.

"Uh . . . this is Norman Gates."

Silence.

"Your mom's here at our house," I pushed on. "They're having a meeting about Fortuna."

"Yeah, I know. She told me."

"I thought . . . well . . ." I suddenly couldn't remember what I thought. Why *was* I calling Lisa?

"What do you think about everybody going to different schools next year?" *There, I got it out.*

"Karen and Sherry and I aren't going to different schools. We'll all be at Clearfield."

"I mean—well—you know—a lot of us will be split up."

"Who, for instance?"

"Steve Pugsley, for instance—and me."

"Oh, *him!*"

But what about you and me, Lisa, my love? I wanted to say it, to bruise her ears with all the feelings exploding inside me, but nothing came out.

Now Lisa was tapping on the phone with her fingernail. I wasn't a bit surprised when she said, "Well, see you tomorrow, okay? I have to go do dinner dishes now."

"Yeah, sure. Nice talking to you."

"Same here," she said.

I hung on for the click. It was over. My first telephone conversation with Lisa was over. I tried to remember what we'd said, but I was so overcome with relief I couldn't concentrate.

"I'm serving coffee, Norman," Mom said as she poked her head in at the door. "Want to pass the refreshments for me? Glenna Pugsley brought a big sack of sweet rolls from the cafe."

I said good-bye to the apple pie I'd been thinking about since dinner and followed her out of the room, wondering how my dad could leave her when she was so pretty. Even in jeans and a turtleneck she was the best-looking mom at the meeting.

Steve and I used to argue over whose mother was cutest, but I still say mine is. She has this fluffy brown hair that curls around her face and a mouth that just automatically turns up at the corners. Dee had a paper doll once that looked just like her. Now, Steve's mother is a totally different type. She's tall and slinky. Seeing them side by side, you might think of a Doberman and a cocker spaniel. I sometimes wondered why they were such good friends, being so different, but I guess Glenna needed Mom to stick

16

up for her in the neighborhood the same way I needed Steve at school.

Anyway, Mrs. Pugsley is a terrific sport, even if she is glamorous. She gets rid of any boyfriend her kids don't like. Dumps them, just like that.

"Hi, Norman," Mrs. Pugsley said when she saw me.

"Hi," I said back.

I stood and watched her arrange the sweet rolls on a tray.

"Steve's really broken up about Fortuna," she said. "I didn't think he gave a hoot about school, did you?"

"Pugs told me he wants to wrestle on the team next year, if there *is* a team."

"It's you, Norman, not the wrestling!" She gave me a perfumy squeeze that I sort of enjoyed.

I smiled. It was true that Steve depended on me for his math and science and sometimes even home ec, but I depended on him, too. His reputation for fighting dirty was great security for my immature ninety-seven-pound frame. Also, Steve was the only person in the world who knew I prayed daily for hormones. Only jockeys and rock-climbers want to stay light. An average kid like me goes for muscles and height.

"Come in and join us, Glenna," Mom said when she returned with the coffeepot. "Norm is fully qualified to pass the treats."

Mrs. Pugsley winked at me.

"I already said you'd be chairperson for one committee," my mother whispered before they headed on into the living room. "Be sure to accept, now. Talk about apathy! Someone needs to build a fire under these deadheads."

17

Too bad Steve had to baby-sit for his twin brothers. Building fires is another one of his specialties.

After everyone left, Mom and I talked while we cleaned up the living room. She told me how we'd all have to pitch in and raise money for a Fortuna fund. Then we'd have to ask for a special meeting of the school board to present our viewpoint. She was full of excited talk, all right, but I wondered whose spirits she was trying to pump up.

After all the dishes were put away, she offered to take me upstairs. "Would you like me to tuck you in? The way I used to? I'll be grading papers until midnight, anyway," she said with a sigh.

That's when I started feeling sorry for her. I was already sorry about Fortuna and about me, but it's a real bone sorrow when you feel that way about your mother. She'd had such high hopes before the meeting. She just *knew* everyone cared as much as she did. Trouble was, they never did.

We started up the stairs in the dark, our arms around each other. I made her stop at the landing, halfway.

"You don't need to come up with me. I'm not a little kid anymore."

"Yes, Normie, I know that. I'm the one who can't kick the habit."

"Hey," I said, putting on the cheer, "why don't we compromise? We'll say good night here. Then you go down and I'll go up."

Laughing, she collapsed on the landing, then pulled me down to sit beside her. "You win." She hugged me and kissed my cheek and ear.

"Say, you need a haircut. Am I neglecting you?"

"No!" How could she see my hair in the dark? I was hoping she'd never notice. Dad was the one who always drove me to the barbershop.

She was quiet all of a sudden, and I knew we were thinking the same thing.

"I wonder what he's doing right now," she said softly. It was starting to be a game with us, wondering what my dad was doing.

"He's probably living it up down there in Mexico City," I said, "drinking margaritas and all that."

"And here we are," Mom sighed again, "propping up a middle school."

She pulled her knees close and rested her chin on her hands. We didn't talk for a minute.

"You still don't understand, do you, Norman?"

"What's to understand?" I croaked. "He wanted to leave, so he left."

I could see her biting her lip, even though the light was dim.

"Norman, listen . . ."

I tried not to. I'd heard it before.

"Your father was simply worn out. He needed a change. I needed a change, too, after eighteen years of being a housewife. We're each doing what we want to do most, which means we have to be apart for the time being. You don't stop accepting challenges just because you're married and have children, you know."

"But *you* didn't run off."

"Your father didn't 'run off.' We've been planning this since last October. Remember the night he came home and told us about Joe and Mary Conrad?"

"Yeah, I remember. You guys talked about it for hours."

19

"Your father promised himself this adventure way back when he was in dental school, then had to postpone it all these years. It was something he had to do. And the time seemed right."

Then her hand grabbed onto mine and I held on, squeezing her fingers until she flinched.

"You know who I love?" she asked in this voice that made me wish I still had a teddy upstairs.

"Yeah . . . only it's supposed to be *whom*."

"*Whom*, then, smartass kid?"

"You love me."

"That's right. You have a good memory. Your dad loves you, too, just as much as I do."

Steve's dad had said the same things before *he* left.

I turned away when she said good night. Was she trying to hide the truth from me? Keep me from knowing until I got used to being without a father?

"Sleep tight," she called after me as I went on up the stairs.

I could have bawled my eyes out right then. We were a family washed up, it seemed to me. Lately I'd found myself envying Steve, of all people. He can slough off his mom's boyfriends like old snakeskin, does it all the time. But you can't slough off your old man.

It was more than Fortuna that crashed down around my ears that tenth day of February. It was my entire terrestrial, tangible world!

5

Everyone was hyper at school the next morning. It was weird. The halls were full of kids long before bell time. People you didn't even know gave you these looks, as if to say, "Ain't it the pits?"

Girls clumped around their lockers, hugging one another. Jan Schmidt and Jan McPhail, who'd been best friends forever, acted like it was Doomsday. The only ones celebrating were some poor, ignorant sixth graders who thought their formal education would now come to an end.

Steve and I had run all the way to school Tuesday morning ourselves. I was working out this plot in my head to kidnap Mr. Gray—with Fortuna being the ransom—but I hadn't told Steve yet. (He's very big on violence.)

Once at school, Pugsley went on to Mr. Donovan's class to copy somebody's homework, so I decided to slip past Lisa Harrington's locker. Casual-like, of course. I was glad she lockered close to the drinking fountain so she wouldn't suspect anything.

Lisa was talking to Diane.

"They have a swimming pool at Clearfield," I heard her say. "I think I'll like it there."

"Lucky you!" Diane moaned. "I'm on a Roy street. But

my dad says he'll get me into Clearfield somehow. Roy Middle School is the cocaine center of the city, did you know that?"

After I'd drunk about a gallon of water, I caught Lisa looking at me. Without recognition, I might add.

I tried smiling. She smiled back at a very fast shutter speed. I cruised on down the hall.

Normal Norman, doomed to get his jollies listening in!

Sometimes I really craved having a heart-to-heart with someone my age besides Steve. Someone female, to be specific.

"I hate those kids at Clearfield," I overheard a skinny sixth grader say. Even *he* was talking to a girl.

"Stuck-up snots," the girl agreed, nice and ladylike.

I moved on toward English, listening to other people's opinions.

"Teachers smoke pot in the men's room over there."

"My cousin told me . . ."

"They give F's at that place!"

"Who cares? I never went to the same school two years in a row yet."

I glanced down the dark locker corridor where the eighth graders go to make out. They weren't wasting any time worrying about the future of Fortuna.

Naturally, in class everyone wanted to talk about the big announcement. Naturally, the teachers didn't.

"School as usual," said Griffin right off, hauling out her pronoun chart. I wondered if the teachers had been threatened with dismissal if they didn't keep their mouths shut.

As the day wore on, we could tell they were just as jumpy as we were. In gym Coach Reese made us run around the building ten times in forty-two-degree weather just because we couldn't shut up during roll call. *He's* the one with the bad nerves. He had two cups of coffee while we were out catching pneumonia. (I know, because Steve checked the indicator on the pot when we got back.)

Then in math Mr. Henry collected only half the homework he'd assigned the day before. He had a real fit. "Displaced anger," my mom would have called it. He couldn't get mad at the school board, so he took it out on us. "You kids want to go back on the computer system?" he raved, using his favorite threat.

Out of all the teachers, only Mrs. Adelsack seemed to understand. She teaches Singles' Survival, which most of us still call home ec. Though we guys were scheduled to make brownies that Tuesday, she started right out by saying, "Okay, you meatheads, let's talk about it. Fortuna's been marked with an *X*. This is *not* the time to try a new recipe." Then she closed the door behind her.

Now, Adelsack's the last person you'd suspect of being radical. She's sixty if she's a day, and her clothes look like they're in a third recycling. But she's quick and smart, and there are rumors that she runs five miles a day. Mostly, after the first shock of seeing her each fall, kids don't notice how she looks.

And no one, *but no one,* leaves the water running or throws out aluminum foil in her kitchen at school.

"Waste is the deadliest sin!" she says, swinging her big yardstick. (Even Pugsley didn't want to get hit with it a second time.)

So there we were, with the district about to waste a perfectly good middle school. We might have known Adelsack would be upending her soapbox.

"Come on, level with me," she said, and slid up onto her

desk, the knees of her polyester pantsuit shining like head-lights. "I mean, what do you really think?"

Cecil Underwood raised his hand.

"I think we need more information before we can make an intelligent decision," he said.

Everyone groaned.

Cecil is too intelligent for his own good. Always safe, he's never going to be sorry in his life. If he'd been there when the British were coming, he'd have asked for a written permission slip before loading his musket. He makes me sick.

"But how do you feel?" Adelsack persisted. "Does closing Fortuna matter to you kids at all?"

Cecil shrugged. "It doesn't matter to me. Getting an education is the important thing. It doesn't matter where."

"Well, I hate it!" Steve said, not even raising his hand.

"Me too," others agreed.

"My dad says we all ought to walk out. Protest or some-thing." That came from Dennis Wagner, who is black and lives straight across from the school. His dad's a lawyer.

"We been together since the beginning," Todd said.

"Yeah, like a family, sort of—"

"Why close school the year we get a good basketball team?"

"Yeah, man—"

"Busing's going to cost lots more, too," Dennis said, "and think of the wasted energy."

"Busing's bullcrap!" from Steve.

Mrs. Adelsack laughed, her wrinkles bunching up around her eyes. "Well, that's reassuring," she said, "you do have feelings about Fortuna. Some of you. Last night was a regular wake in the faculty room. The teachers had the school dead and buried without even giving it a funeral. I walked right out, I was so disgusted."

No one else would have told us that. What went on in the faculty room was top-priority secret stuff.

Mrs. Adelsack got down from where she was perched and pulled a pan of brownies out of an oven. (I thought I'd smelled brownies!) When she started cutting them in squares, we looked at one another and raised our eyebrows. She went right on talking over the gurgling sounds of our gastric juices.

"Ten years ago Fortuna was built to take students from Southridge Elementary, which was also a neighborhood school. Our little community was sort of isolated then, wasn't it? We were the dog's tail not long ago . . . a growing suburb . . . away from the city. A nuisance to the district, really. So"—she rinsed and dried her hands—"they built Southridge and Fortuna, and all the kids were able to walk to school. Now what's happening? Why is the enrollment down all of a sudden?"

"No more babies."

"Families growing up, kids leaving," said someone else.

"We shouldn't of sent in that census," Steve growled. "I knew we shouldn't of."

Don Marsh laughed right out loud until he saw Mrs. Adelsack pull out her spatula. He quit laughing at once.

"What happens when kids leave home for good?" Adelsack asked as she lifted brownies out of the pan and onto a plate. "Your folks going to keep those nice big *empty* houses?"

"My parents are moving into a condominium," Cecil said smugly, "to be nearer the university."

"Exactly!" Adelsack nodded. "And who will buy those three- and four-bedroom homes?"

"People with kids!" Bob and Greg said together.

"Why can't the school board figure that out?" I asked.

"There's a budget squeeze going on, Norman. Inflation!" She spit out the word. "And we all get a little shortsighted from time to time. But I don't think Fortuna is a lost cause . . . no siree, I don't."

She handed out napkins and passed the plate of brownies among the dozen or so guys in the room.

"Take two, boys, they're small."

You can see how an old girl like that held her own in middle school. She'd never be voted Popularity Plus or Miss Let's-Be-Pals, but she understood guys. The other home ec teacher had her kids making aprons, for crying out loud. Not Adelsack. Our first-semester sewing project was a stuff bag for backpacking.

She never asked us to make oatmeal or cinnamon toast or any of that easy stuff, either. We fixed jerky and hero sandwiches and made campfire pizza in the teachers' lounge fireplace.

Lessons in her class were never dull, either. "Seven Shortcuts to Table Setting" turned out to be more like baseball practice. Two cups and a saucer were broken before we got the hang of it.

By the time school let out that day, I'd come to several conclusions: (1) The students were of two opinions. Either they cared about Fortuna or they didn't, same as their parents. (2) The teachers had been brainwashed. They'd do as they were told. All except Adelsack the Hun, as we called her on occasion. (3) Lisa Harrington would come to know of my existence. (4) I had to quit worrying about my dad.

Steve liked to watch the wrestling team work out every Tuesday, so I walked home by myself that night. It was beginning to snow again—soft, airy flakes that melted on my face. Pretty soon I caught myself whistling that song about dreaming the impossible dream and fighting the unbeatable foe.

Suddenly, right there on the sidewalk, walking along by myself, I broke out laughing. What a kooky picture I was getting in my head! It was Adelsack and she was slashing the air with her yardstick, a crazy-lady Don Quixote, attacking this unsuspecting windmill.

"Take that, and *that*, you shortsighted monster!"

I couldn't stop laughing. I felt positively wonderful after having that vision.

6

te na cious—adj., holding fast, persistent, stubborn

te nac i ty—n., the quality of being tenacious

"But what's the difference?" I asked Mom as she sat at the table, blow-drying her hair and eating toast at the same time.

"What did you say?" she shouted.

"—the difference, between those words. I don't get it."

"Tenacity is what you have if you're tenacious," she grinned, catching my sister's long hair in the breeze of the dryer.

"He's such a pea brain, why do you bother?" Dee said.

Mom didn't hear that. She was craning around to see the kitchen clock. "Oh look, I'm late again!"

"So what's new?" my sister mumbled.

She talks back a lot while Mom is drying her hair. One of these days she's going to get caught.

I was still thinking about the words on the fridge when Mom switched off the dryer. I knew if I got her talking about the new vocabulary words, she might stay home awhile longer.

"You're always telling me I'm stubborn, Mom. Maybe what I am is ten*a*cious."

"No, Normie," Dee said, "you're just plain stubborn."

"Delilah!"

Mom turned back to me. "If this PTA committee raises enough money to conduct a study on Fortuna and hire a lawyer both, we'll consider ourselves *tenacious!*"

She leaned across the table to kiss each of us. I could smell her shampoo, which was the same as Lisa's.

"Faculty meeting this morning, I have to go early. Do the dishes and don't give Animal your cornflakes, Norman." (The truth is, our big shaggy mutt likes cornflakes better than I do.)

Right after the announcement about Fortuna, the PTA decided to mount a campaign against the school board. Suddenly everyone was out to raise money so we could make a good case for keeping Fortuna open. The PTA committee would need flyers, ads, postage, a return-address rubber stamp—all that kind of stuff. The most expensive item would be lawyer's fees. My mom said the PTA would definitely need legal advice.

My dad always bragged about Mom being a good manager, but when the jobs were passed out, she ended up being the busing chairperson. Glenna Pugsley got to be the chief fund-raiser.

In the meantime at school the different classes decided to have a competition to see who could raise the most money. The stupid seventh grade—my class, naturally—which stood to gain the most if Fortuna stayed open, had so far raised the least. Which was nothing. Zero dollars and zero cents!

The sixth graders got in gear first. With fireball Glenna

29

Pugsley organizing things, they held a Saturday-morning Kite Kompetition the first week of March. Thirty-four sixth graders and their dads showed up. (The little Pugsley twins were there too, but their "dad" was Glenna's boyfriend. I believe this one's name was Charles.)

Thirty-four kids and thirty-odd dads makes sixty-some dollars just for the entrance fee. By the time the kite-flyers bought apple pie, doughnuts, nachos, and drinks, the sixth graders had skimmed nearly two hundred bucks off their dads.

Mrs. Pugsley had arranged for the kite-flying to start out near the pine grove at one end of the Little League field. I think she knew the "repair and replacement shack"—a van parked nearby—would do a good business with all those kites getting tangled up in the trees and with each other. (I heard the shack also carried oxygen for fathers who might need resuscitation.)

All in all the little old sixth graders raised $227, and Glenna Pugsley returned home with a new boyfriend. I don't know what happened to Charles.

The eighth graders earned even more money, though they were the ones leaving Fortuna behind. I think Coach Reese was the reason. He didn't want to commute to Roy or Clearfield. He lives only two blocks from Fortuna Middle School.

Anyway, the eighth-grade basketball team played a benefit game against the faculty men and women one night. The gym was packed. And guess who was the high scorer for the ladies? It wasn't Miss Griffin, who has these terrific legs, or Gwen Pepper, the drama coach who looks like Bo Derek. It was Adelsack, playing ball in a 1920s gym suit—bloomers

30

and middy. You should have heard the howls when she jogged out on the floor with first-stringers Reese, Donovan, Henry, and Clayton.

Of course, Adelsack didn't get the ball very much, but when she got it, she scored. She wasn't too shabby on defense, either. How would it feel to be out there with those skinny arms waving over you as you tried to break free? It gives me the shivers!

In all, she played about four minutes of game time. Krepps and Hansen laughed so hard when she was on the floor, they almost lost the ball game for the students. But not quite.

At half time the cheerleaders held a bake sale in the corridor outside the gym. Pugs and I spent a whole week's allowance (mine) on fudge and cream puffs. In fifteen minutes the table was as empty as Bogucki's Bakery on a Saturday night.

When the eighth grade announced its earnings at the end of the game, the grand total was around $350. You should have heard the cheers *then*!

For some reason we seventh graders couldn't come up with any ideas. We had a meeting in the auditorium that got exactly nowhere. First someone suggested we have a bike wash. How dumb can you get! I could just see the Pugsley twins pumping up to the school grounds on their dirt bikes, dimes clutched in their sticky little palms.

Then Diane and a bunch of girls who were likewise doomed to attend Roy Middle School stood up and proposed a garage sale. They'd do the advertising and everything if we'd come and bring our stuff.

Everyone voted for that, but it didn't work out. It rained

all day that Saturday and nobody showed up. Aside from my old games and Steve's collection of firearms (a rubber-band shooter, a Davy Crockett side arm, and a BB gun that almost worked), very little was brought to the sale. Five of us sat around in Diane's garage all morning, keeping an eye on the neighbor kids who only came to finger Steve's guns.

Everyone got cold and crabby. By noon we'd earned the grand total of $2.05 for the PTA. We'd sold one pair of sunglasses, an old sweater of Diane's, and a pickle dish that went for 5 cents to a stranger.

When we accused Diane of forgetting to put the ad in the paper, she burst out crying. We knew then she hadn't done it, so we took our stuff and went home.

The next meeting we had was at Lisa Harrington's after school. She and Sherry and Karen were all hot on having a seventh-grade amateur hour and charging admission.

Pugsley doubled up laughing. "Who's going to pay to hear you play the piano, Lisa?"

"Shut up!" she ordered. (She's very up front with Steve.)

I didn't know what the other two girls had in mind. Sherry does gymnastics on nearly every assembly we have at school. The kids wouldn't pay to see her perform when she was all the time doing it for free. And Karen doesn't have any talents that I know about. She does raise tropical fish, but what can a tropical fish do in a talent show?

There were eight of us there, with Lisa and Sherry having the only talents, so that idea was voted down.

Then Greg suggested we walk people's dogs. He'd read about this kid in a book who walked dogs for money.

"Animal's so old I have to pay him to take walks," I said, though Lisa gave me a dirty look for opening my mouth.

Anyway, that idea didn't go over either. Lisa especially couldn't get excited about it. She still wanted to perform her new Sonata on everyone.

Finally the meeting broke up. I felt really sorry for Lisa. She was disappointed as anything.

I got up my courage and hung back behind the others to speak to her. "Look . . . I'll try to come up with something."

"*You?* You don't have any ideas. You just vote down other people's!"

"No, honest, that's not true!" I shoved my hands in my pockets, thinking how true it was. "I was just . . . out of it tonight." I'd been distracted, for sure. Lisa has these naturally red cheeks and lips, and this shiny brown hair with the flipped ends. How could I come up with anything sitting across the rec room from her?

"I promise. Count on me." I was really laying myself on the line.

Lisa folded a stick of gum in her mouth and began to chew. But she didn't go back in the house, even though it was chilly outside. She just leaned against the porch railing staring at Steve. He was out on the driveway waiting for me, demolishing the girls with his charm, but I didn't make a move to leave.

Finally, Lisa turned and looked at me. "See here, Norman Gates! I want to run for eighth-grade secretary, but if we don't come up with a good idea for raising money, Elaine Tucker's friends *will*. Do you want to stand by me or let all those kids get in office again next year?"

"I'm with you, honest!"

"Then break your brain on it! We need an idea!" She

turned and marched back into the house, her clogs making exclamation points behind her.

I was grinning like a hyena when I caught up with the others.

"She's one tenacious girl," I said to Steve, who's always impressed with my vocabulary. "I mean, she's got *tenacity*!"

"You can say that again," Steve agreed.

But when I tried to, he stuck his fist in my mouth. (Steve will only put up with so much.)

7

A letter from my dad had been sitting in the mailbox all afternoon and no one knew it. I carried it into the house on top of the Frostline catalog and the light bill.

Ms. Barbara Gates, it said. There was no *and family* on this one.

"Some things bear looking into," my mother told me the day Steve and I read Mr. Clayton's letter when we shouldn't have. However, a letter from my dad addressed to my mom wasn't exactly the same as a dittoed message from school.

I was itching to open it but figured a peanut butter sandwich would help me make up my mind. The end-of-cafeteria bell had rung halfway through my bowl of chili, as usual, and just being with Lisa had revved up my metabolism something awful.

I took my sandwich and milk to the table, propped the letter against Mom's centerpiece of dried weeds, and stared at it. I wondered if I'd ever get a letter from him addressed to me. To me alone.

Mr. Norman M. Gates. Or better yet, *Personal: for Norman Gates Himself.*

The letter might read:

Dear Son,

Your mother and I made a big mistake when we decided I'd go on this climbing trip. I'm here in the hospital in Mexico City with a stubborn case of heat rash and it looks like I'll have to call everything off. Tell your mother she can go on working if she likes it so much. We aren't going to fight about that anymore. Also, I'm thinking of buying you the new Miyata ten-speed when I get home. Every boy should have a racing bike. I sure miss all of you. Especially you, Norm, old buddy. Don't know what I was thinking about, not taking my best climbing partner along. Next summer we'll do Mount Rainier together, okay?

It was a lie. All of it. Even the Rainier part. Dad had promised Mom he wouldn't take me up there until I was sixteen.

The letter in front of me probably said something more like:

Dear Mrs. Gates:

The divorce papers are being drawn up now. These Mexican lawyers don't mess around. Please sign both copies and return mine. You can have the house, the cars, the dog, and the kids. My freedom will be enough for me. Adios, amigos!

Formerly yours,
Michael Gates, D.D.S.

Just then Dee burst in the front door. Jennifer was with her and they'd been talking about boys. I can always tell because they fall into this fakey silence when they see me.

"Oh, *you*'re home," Dee said, making me feel about as cherished as a case of Legionnaire's disease. "I thought you had a meeting after school."

"I did."

"Hey, we got a letter from Dad!" She picked up the envelope, read it, set it down again. "Where's Mom?"

"Out riding the city bus. You're supposed to make dinner."

"Oh, cripes! Why's she riding the bus?"

Good question, I was thinking as I carried my dishes to the sink. I'd have given anything right then to back up and start the whole crazy year over again.

"Norman, answer me! Why's she riding the bus?"

"She's the busing chairperson, can't you remember anything?"

"Is he making any sense to you?" Dee asked Jennifer, who had opened the fridge and was making herself at home.

"No," she answered, "but does he ever?"

I hated them equally.

"She's interviewing the bus driver," I shouted, "and observing! The school board says it can bus us *off* the Fortuna hill in the winter but that it wouldn't be safe to bus kids *in* to Fortuna. Mom's out to prove they're liars."

"My mother, the crusader!" Dee made a fist over her heart. "I hope I live through this, it's so embarrassing."

She'd have been really embarrassed if she could have seen into the future as far as May. She might even have left home, like my dad did. (I'd have savored that idea then—Dee leaving home, for any reason.)

Just then the telephone rang. I beat my sister to it, thinking maybe Lisa was calling. Now that we'd had a real conversation . . . maybe it was Lisa!

37

"Hello? Norman Gates speaking."

It was one of Dad's patients, asking when Dr. Gates would be back in the office. She had just chipped a front tooth.

"Dr. Amatio is seeing my father's patients," I said. "His number is 287-4414." I had the speech memorized. Hundreds had heard it already. *Why couldn't it have been Lisa?*

Then this lady went on to tell me how she'd put on her daughter's roller skates, "just fooling around, you know . . ."

Yeah, yeah.

"Suddenly my feet went out from under me and now I have this fat lip and a tooth that looks like a fang . . ."

All the while she was talking, I was getting this wonderful idea. The seventh grade could sponsor a roller derby! In the school parking lot! We could have music and couples' numbers. I saw Lisa . . . skating with me . . . my arm around her waist . . .

"Are you still there?" the voice asked.

"Uh—yes, ma'am, I'm still here."

"When will Dr. Gates be back in his office?"

"We don't know for sure. In June, I guess."

"Well, thank you, young man. You've been . . . most helpful."

So have you!

I hung up, reached for the phone book, and flipped to the Yellow Pages. Karen's tropical fish hadn't suggested anything at all, but what we'd forgotten that afternoon was that Karen's father owned the skate rental at Ebony Park. This time of year he'd be begging for business.

Boldly, I picked up the phone and dialed Ebony Park Rentals and Repairs.

"May I speak to Mr. Hartzinger, please?" I said in this well-modulated voice. "Yes, this is a business call."

Dee's mouth fell open and Jennifer stared. (Personally, I was hearing that trumpeter again. The one on the parapet, remember?)

8

Mom didn't get home from her bus excursion until after six that night. I met her at the door, waving Dad's letter overhead.

"Guess what came in the mail?"

"A letter from Michael!" she guessed, practically snatching it out of my hands.

We'd had one postcard from Mexico City, where members of his climbing group met, and another from a village with an unpronounceable name. *This* was the first real letter.

We were all so excited, in fact, that Dee let the tomato soup burn. Now, there's no smell worse than stuck-to-the-pan tomato soup, unless it's the putrefying smell of an egg boiled dry. With Dee cooking part time, we'd experienced both.

"It's okay, forget it," Mom said when Dee started screaming about how it was all my fault. Quickly, Mom turned on the kitchen fan.

"Burned soup is Animal's favorite," she said. "Let's eat at the drive-in tonight and we'll read Daddy's letter afterward. We'll celebrate the occasion, okay?"

"Oh, no," I groaned, "you're not gonna make us wait!"

"I'm a *mean* mother!" she said, grinning right into my face.

(My mother celebrates everything—a full moon, the last payment on her VISA card, the first crocus. We had to burn candles on the dinner table the day her orneriest D student made an A on his poetry test, of all things!)

Mom poured the burny soup mess into Animal's dog dish and added a handful of oyster crackers, the way he likes it. Then she disappeared into the bathroom. I had the feeling she wanted to read Dad's letter first, to doctor it up and soften the bad news for us. I also remembered that the bathroom is the one place you can go if you have to cry.

But her eyes weren't the least bit red when we left for McDonald's five minutes later, and the letter was still unopened in her hand.

"Next time you ride the bus all over the place, let me know earlier," Dee said in the car, still mad about the soup. "Jennifer was here and everything. I could have made a really good dinner if you'd told me sooner."

"Yeah, we could have had cordon bleu," I said.

"Shut up! Who asked you to butt in?"

"I should wait for an invitation? 'In thirty seconds, Norman, you may butt in. . . .' "

Dee gave me this slit-eyed look over her shoulder. "Do you know what he did tonight?"

I couldn't wait to hear what I'd done.

"Is this necessary?" Mom interrupted. "Would you kids be bickering like this if Daddy were along?"

"If Dad was here, she'd be in the backseat hitting me instead of *slandering* me!"

Mom laughed, which made Dee even madder. By the time we got to the drive-in, we looked good and snarly, like any other fatherless American family going out for hamburgers.

41

"Now keep it within reason," Mom said as we walked in to order, which is what she always says—automatically. (1) Open the door at McDonald's. (2) Voice says "Keep it within reason." (3) Stomachs growl in protest. That's the sequence with Mom.

When Dad used to take us out, he'd say, "Is that all you want?" Or "Make those drinks large, why don't you?" Sometimes he'd add his own personal touch to what we'd ordered: "Throw in a cherry pie there," he'd say, like he was Howard Hughes or some big millionaire.

"Remember, Norman," Mom said, her paranoia rising, "we're living on my salary for a while. Order just what you can eat."

Ordering "what I could eat" was out of the question. I wouldn't dare do that!

During dinner, seated at a table inside, Mom told us about her bus ride. She'd timed the city bus going up the Fortuna hill, coming down the Fortuna hill. She'd asked the driver how many times the transit service *hadn't* been able to make the round trip this winter because of bad weather.

"What did he say?" Dee asked to one side of her malt straw.

"Exactly one time!" Mom replied with smoke billowing out of her ears. "Who do they think we are? Idiots? 'No, we won't consider busing from overcrowded schools into Fortuna,' the board says. 'It isn't safe or dependable during the winter months.' Hogwash!"

"I know another word you could use—" I said, trying to be helpful, but Mom covered my mouth with a napkin.

Then Dee started talking about the girls'-choice dance that was coming up, wondering if she should ask Dave

Pfeiffer—who has these overdeveloped muscles but no brains—or Bill Perry, who is such a terrific dancer and dresser.

"Bill asked you to the Valentine's Dance," Mom said, "why don't you ask him back?"

"His face is still peeling," Dee replied dreamily, "from falling asleep under his dad's sun lamp. I may ask this new kid, except he might be shorter than me. I'll stand by him tomorrow and have Jennifer check."

Mom smiled at me. I sat there, listening, eating slowly, dragging the meal out. I wanted to hear Dad's letter, but I didn't. Everything seemed so kind of normal for a change. Kind of everyday-ish. As long as you don't know for a fact that something is so . . . it isn't so, is it?

They were both finished way ahead of me. Dee left to comb her hair in the ladies' and Mom got a refill on her coffee. Finally, I washed down the last french fry with Coke and wiped the grease off my fingers.

Mom pulled the letter out of her purse then and slit it open with the handle of a plastic spoon. Miraculously, Dee stopped talking about herself. I took a deep breath and crossed my fingers under the table.

"Dearest Barbara," the letter began. Mom looked up. "That includes you two, of course."

Who was she kidding? If he'd wanted to include us, he'd have said so. He knew how to spell our names.

"I found your welcome letters waiting for me at the American Express when we got back to Mexico City. I turned down dinner with Brady and the others so I could write and post a reply before we fly out of here in the morning. From now on, it will be difficult to get messages to you,

43

so please, honey, don't worry. 'No news is good news,' right? I know now why that adage has been perpetuated. Already I'm feeling out of touch—out of reach—of you and the family. . . ."

Mom stopped there and her eyes swept ahead through the next part of the letter. When she finished, the look on her face told us she'd momentarily been south of the border. "That part was for me," she said softly.

The next page was telling Mom not to forget the car insurance payment. Also, "be sure to get Animal his rabies shot. It's due before April 30. And next time you talk to Dr. Amatio, ask him to—"

My mind wandered. Here he'd gone on this sabbatical, as we were supposed to call it, to get away from the dental practice, and his first letter home was full of it. He was more worried about how some old guy's dentures were fitting than he was about us!

Suddenly, I heard my name mentioned. "I'll bet Norman's started that growth spurt by now."

Sorry, Dad, it hasn't happened.

"The size of those feet indicates substantial growth ahead. Help him to be patient, if you have to."

I looked down at my size nine Nikes. He was right. My feet were too big for the rest of me.

"I hope Delilah's making the most of her sophomore year. Don't tell her that's the age you and I started going steady, Barb. But I guess kids have better sense than that now."

Dee wrinkled her nose. "I can't afford to go steady on *my* allowance."

I was busy reading between the lines. That comment, *kids have better sense these days*, was a dig at Mom, a real dig.

Knowing what he knows now, Dad probably wouldn't have got married at all. And where would I be if he hadn't? I'd be a nonmolecular nonentity, that's what! Free-floating atoms of carbon and nitrogen and hydrogen . . .

"Tell Norman"—my ears perked up like Animal's when he hears the crackle of cellophane—"we needed crampons and ice axes both on Orizaba's north slope. Brady experienced some altitude sickness, but I made it with little discomfort. It was an exhilarating climb. Standing at 18,700 feet is a heady experience."

The rest of the letter was a schedule of where he'd be and when. Not that we could reach him! "We'll be in Nepal the end of May if all goes well. I'll call home as often as I get a chance," he said.

So far his only call had come when Dee and I were in bed asleep.

Then Mom was at the end of the letter and suddenly she quit reading. Tears filled her eyes. She handed it to Dee, grabbed my hand, and hung on until she got control again. Right there in front of all those people, she semi broke down. I have to admit I felt very funny about it.

Dee went ahead and read the ending out loud.

I still can't understand what got Mom so choked up all of a sudden. "I see you in the sunrise" was all it said.

9

> **Fortuna's Seventh Grade Proudly Presents**
> **FOOLS ON WHEELS**
> A Roller Derby for young and old—
> Students, Teachers, Parents, Grandparents,
> Cousins, Uncles, and even
> Principal types!!
>
> **MUSIC, FUN, FOOD!**
> April 1, 7:00 to 9:00 P.M.
> School Parking Lot
> One dollar will get you rollin', no foolin'!

Steve, Karen, Sherry, and I made the posters, but Lisa read the announcement. Every day for a week she read it on the PA. When April Fools' Friday finally rolled around, Fortuna's hottest topic was the seventh-grade fund-raiser.

"Go with me to the derby tonight?" the sixth-grade boys were saying to the sixth-grade girls. Then "April fool!" they'd scream and fall over laughing when the girls said yes.

Even the teachers acted as if it was a real holiday. For

once there was no homework assigned. Everyone seemed real cheerful, too, considering it was Friday and teachers' wit's-end day.

Mrs. Adelsack, especially, got right into the spirit of things. She had the Singles' Survival class making spiced cider on Wednesday, popping corn on Thursday. On Friday we bagged caramel corn in these little sacks that had "Fortuna Foolfaddle" printed on one side. (The bags were courtesy of Glenna Pugsley, whose new boyfriend works at a print shop.)

With everything depending on it, the weather that night turned out to be perfect. Spring smell was everywhere. The air felt soft, almost slippery, if you know what I mean. I could imagine how it would be skating with Lisa, the breezes rippling over our faces, the clear night carrying our laughter all the way to the stars.

The committee who dreamed it all up—Steve, Lisa, Karen, Sherry, and yours truly—had to be there by six. Steve and I were so hyper we ran the entire distance back to school. Good thing, too. There was plenty to do getting ready. Karen Hartzinger helped her dad organize the skates by sizes in the back of his pickup. Steve and I hauled tables and benches out of the cafeteria so skaters could sit down and have someplace to leave their shoes. Lisa and Sherry gave Adelsack a hand setting up refreshments in the court between the gym and the classroom building.

Somehow, Adelsack had conned the nearby 7-Eleven into providing a microwave oven and about fifty dollars' worth of pizza. "Pure profit," she chortled, rolling out an extension cord for the microwave. "Yes siree! The merchants will chip in if it means saving the school."

Steve and I couldn't help laughing about the way she was

dressed for the derby. She was wearing these bright green sweats under a pair of greenish yellow gym shorts. In all that green, with her elbows and heels hiking up at the same time, she looked exactly like a grasshopper. Steve noticed the resemblance at once.

At six thirty the parking lot lights went on. Kids were starting to buy tickets out in the drive, where two PTA ladies were selling them at the tailgate of a station wagon. At a buck apiece we'd be taking in more than a little cash!

By starting time Coach Reese had marked off a big oval skateway with the white stuff they use on the football field. Across the court Adelsack had strung Japanese lanterns that winked on and off like pink and orange fireflies. When Sherry put on the first disco tape and turned up the volume, we were in a fool's paradise for sure. "I'd Love You If You'd Let Me" pulsed through the night air—Fortuna's very own heartbeat. Our school was a living, breathing organism! Why wasn't the school board able to see that?

At seven I got Lisa and we jogged out to where ropes closed off the driveway. Steve and I had arranged it so Lisa and I would take tickets the first half hour. That way I'd have a chance to ask her to skate before the other guys did.

I moved a sawhorse aside so we'd face each other across a narrow opening. I couldn't believe it, but the first thing Lisa did was smile at me.

"This was a terrific idea, Norman," she said, her red cheeks making dimples. "I'm glad you thought of it."

"Thanks," I said in this humble voice.

I was trying to think of something nice to say back, but our conversation ended there. In two seconds I couldn't even see her for the kids pushing past us.

Everyone was squealing and excited. The eighth graders, naturally, got rowdy, calling each other fools and pranking around. Gary Wannamaker, this big jock Steve admires who is on the wrestling team, said, "Hey, Norman, your fly's open." Naturally I checked. I was so high that night, I could have forgotten to put on my jeans.

"April fool!" he howls, his loud yuks carrying all the way across the lot. I was glad then that Lisa couldn't see my face.

In spite of stupid old Wannamaker I was just beginning to think the school board's decision might not be a hundred percent bad. It had brought Lisa and me together on this committee. It had sort of brought Karen and Steve together, too. At least he'd been taking a lot of baths lately, his mom told mine, and I noticed him staring at Karen Hartzinger whenever he had a chance. He was probably out there skating with her now, lucky dog.

I couldn't wait to have my turn with Lisa, but people kept arriving right through the first twenty minutes.

We didn't get any grandparents on skates, but a few parents tried it. My mom begged off to do her grocery shopping and catch up on the wash, but Glenna Pugsley showed up with her boyfriend the printer. Naturally, the twins were tagging along with them.

"I may need a lesson," she said to me, "when will you be through here, Norman?"

Oh, no!

"Steve's out there skating now," Lisa said, saving me. "I saw him."

I smiled broadly. "Yeah, Steve will prop you up, Mrs. Pugsley."

"Raymond here says he'd rather watch," Glenna said,

poking this new guy in the ribs. "Can you believe anyone being such a spoilsport?"

She snapped her gum and he rolled his eyes up toward the brim of his cowboy hat. The twins had run on ahead, noisily smacking the pavement with their sneakers.

"I'll corral you later, Normie," Mrs. Pugsley said as she threatened me with a wink.

"Does she think she's going to a rodeo, or what?" Lisa said, kind of snide-like. I thought Glenna looked pretty terrific in the pink and silver outfit that matched her boyfriend's shirt.

Dee came late with Jennifer, hoping some high school guys would be hanging around, no doubt. In fact, they didn't buy tickets for a while, just stood outside the chain link fence casing things. Finally they paid and came on in. Dee didn't speak to me, though Lisa got a "hi" out of her. In public she pretends we're not related.

I was just getting up my nerve for some small talk with Lisa when she spoke up ahead of me.

"Would you care if I got Steve over here to help you? It's slowing down, and I promised Jeff Calavari I'd meet him at seven thirty."

Jeff Calavari! He's an eighth grader, for crying out loud. Why does she want to meet him?

Sure enough, there was Jeff, walking toward us, his broad shoulders straining at the seams of his sweater, his thumbs hooked in his jeans pockets. Your all-American type. Jeff doesn't even have zits!

He nodded at Lisa, very cool-like.

"How's it going, Norm?" he says to me.

I answer something.

50

Lisa didn't wait for me to say "okay" or "toughshitski" or *anything!*

"I'll send Steve over," she says, her eyes all sparkling. "Thanks loads, Norman."

Her brown hair bounced on her shoulders as she walked away. She was looking up at Jeff the way a puppy dog looks at its master.

I stood there alone, choking with disappointment.

Where's the new Norman Gates now, huh? Where's that snappy, aggressive Idea Man who's been swaggering around the halls of Fortuna these last weeks?

I couldn't decide whether Steve ought to beat up Gary Wannamaker or pulverize Jeff Calavari. I felt myself getting a headache, even though my favorite song was filling the night air.

After about six more months of taking tickets by myself, Steve and Karen skated up to take over.

"Why'd you let him ace you out?" Steve whispered as Karen skated beyond us to talk to the PTA ladies.

I shrugged.

Steve leaned on the sawhorse and kicked his skates against the asphalt. "Maybe he should have a little accident," he said, this sinister smile settling on his mouth.

I could picture Lisa going off in the ambulance with Jeff, holding his hand, kissing his smooth, zit-free brow.

"Forget it, Pugs, it wouldn't work."

"I'll go help Adelsack awhile," I said. *Maybe I'll poison Jeff's pizza,* I was thinking.

"Hey," Steve called after me, "get some skates on, will ya? You and me . . . we'll show 'em how it's done."

I walked off, thinking what a good friend Steve was. I had

to admit I was feeling jealous, with everything working out so well for him.

I stopped and asked Mr. Hartzinger to save me a pair of size nines, but I wasn't sure I wanted to skate now. I wasn't about to do a couples' number with Steve!

A bunch of girls stumbled past me, laughing their heads off and hanging on to one another. Beginners, obviously. Sherry went by, slick as glass, waving and skating backward. The rest of the skaters were one big blur, accompanied by the sounds of rumbling rollers and throbbing music. I couldn't see Lisa anywhere. Jeff either. But somewhere, among all those kids circling the parking lot, Jeff was holding Lisa's hand and smiling into Lisa's brown eyes.

Adelsack, at least, was glad to see me when I showed up in the court.

"Don't think anyone ate dinner," she muttered, hopping between the microwave and the lineup of hungry customers.

Dennis Wagner was tending the hot-cider dispenser. Cecil Underwood was selling Fortuna Foolfaddle. Cecil may be stuck on himself, but you have to admire him for the way he makes change. "—thirty-five, forty, and that makes fifty," he'd say, counting out money like the president of Chase Manhattan Bank.

"What I need is someone with muscle," Adelsack told me.

I was about to go get Steve when she handed me the knife and pointed to a cutting board on the table.

"See that stack of pizzas? They're still half frozen. Cut them in fourths first, then eighths—all the way through the bottom crust. Set each section on a paper plate."

The dinger on the oven went off and she whisked out these slices of Fortuna's Finest. The cheese was bubbling. Steamo-

52

Italiano rose to my nostrils. My stomach served notice on my brain then, and I decided Jeff and Lisa Harrington could have each other. For tonight, anyway. Besides, what could I do about it? Saving Fortuna was a big enough assignment for an average kid like me.

10

The Easter bunny must have known we were having a crisis at our house. He just hopped right on by.

Steve and the twins fared way better than the Gates family. When we met the Pugsleys at the Pancake House for Easter brunch, all the little boys could talk about was their overprivileged Easter baskets.

Our own mother hardly knew what day it was. She was still licking her wounds from the way the school board had treated her and the other PTA members.

"I just feel defeated," Mom told Mrs. Pugsley after we'd all ordered.

"Likewise," said Steve's mom, who sat with her chin propped on both hands.

Nobody except the twins had the Easter spirit.

"Wouldn't a lawyer know what to do?" Dee asked, worming her way into the adult conversation.

"Probably," Mrs. Pugsley nodded, "at seventy-five dollars an hour."

"We've used half the money already," Mom said, "just getting the facts before the board. And what good did it do?" (*Half* the money was over four hundred bucks. We'd really cleaned up on the Roller Derby, taking in $6.80 more than the eighth graders did.)

I felt gloomy, too, remembering how hard the PTA committee had worked. How hard *we*'d worked, passing out hand bills at the supermarket, conducting this door-to-door preschool age survey and having Mr. Crampton sic his dog on us.

I also remembered the night Lisa Harrington and I were out measuring the grade of the Fortuna hill by flashlight to get the facts for Mom's busing committee. It started to snow on us and we started laughing, slipping and sliding around. Lisa said, "Let's go to my house and make popcorn when we finish." I couldn't believe my own ears. And then Jeff Calavari came by. Lisa's memory failed rapidly once she saw him, and I ended up walking home by myself.

"I hate like everything to agree with that old sourpuss Morris Sweitzer," Mom said, breaking into my thoughts, "but I think he's right. Shared usage is our answer."

"What's 'shared usage'?" Dee asked, pretending to be interested.

"That's having someone else share the building. And the costs of keeping it open," Mom said. "Like having a renter, sort of."

"Who'd want to rent Fortuna?" Steve asked, peering at me from under his scraggly hair.

"God knows!" said Glenna Pugsley. "Maybe a private school . . . or . . . or something equally impossible for us to come up with in the few weeks they're giving us."

Mom rolled her eyes to the ceiling and spread her hands. "Where are you, Michael, now that I need you?"

Mom was starting to say things like that. She was trying to be funny, but I knew that deep inside she meant it. It made me madder than ever at my dad, who was off climbing molehills while Mom and I were left facing real mountains.

"Like Mildred Fensley says"—Mom wasn't to be side-tracked—"it would be great having a branch of the public library in Fortuna. Trouble is, what can we do in a month?"

"Who needs more books?" Steve said. "I'm already going blind from reading."

"Me too," agreed the twins, who had barely learned how. Then the pancakes arrived and the little kids battled over the syrups.

"I want the blue one—"

"Gimme coconut!"

"Norman, would you please pass the honey?" Dee's voice sailed disdainfully over our heads so the teen-age boy clearing tables would hear. She didn't want to be classed with the rest of us, that's for sure.

I just sat there and bisected my sausages, thinking. If Fortuna was going to try for a renter, it ought to be someone the students would support. A business, maybe. Not another school or library!

I went over the business possibilities in my mind. I thought of a bike shop . . . Raleigh Racers . . . Miyata Sales and Repair . . . Heck, I'd dropped thirty bucks at Schwinn Cyclery since September trying to keep my old junior ten-speed rolling! Think how much all the kids together might spend!

Or how about a Baskin-Robbins? Fortuna's Forty-one Flavors! That would go over big.

Next I thought about a movie theater that showed all G's —Walt Disneys, wildlife adventures, cartoons and stuff. I was getting all worked up over that idea when I caught Mom looking at me.

"Norman, your pancakes are getting cold. Are you feeling all right?"

"He's thinking about Lisa Harrington," Dee said.

"Nah, he hates her guts," Steve said. Which was what I told Steve when Lisa wouldn't skate with me and I ended up being Adelsack's partner for the couples' contest.

I didn't let their small talk distract me. Already I'd crossed out the idea of a neighborhood movie house. Old Mr. Trotter, the janitor, would have cardiac arrest at the sight of all that popcorn under the seats. He was the one who'd be glad if the school closed. "Should have retired last spring," he always muttered if you had a jammed locker.

But I wasn't giving up. The grown-ups needed some input. If the parents couldn't get anywhere with the school board, maybe the kids could.

I poured maple syrup over my stack of pancakes and dug in. I vowed I'd have an idea by the time I could see the plate again. "Break your brain on it, Buster!" came Lisa's voice from afar.

Apparently that did it. I was suddenly having this creative breakthrough. There on my plate, instead of the spreading maple syrup, I was seeing this fake vomit. Dennis Wagner had put fake vomit on Gary Wannamaker's cafeteria tray after the big wrestler had called him a nigger one day. The following week at school plastic vomit turned up everywhere, along with doggie-do and other unmentionable imitations.

I kept on eating, but secretly I was smiling. The grown-ups would never consider renting space to the Merriweather Novelty Co. precisely because their minds didn't work that way. But I was your average, run-of-the-mill twelve-year-old kid, and I knew instinctively that a trick shop at Fortuna would be a hundred times more popular than an old library. Why, Merriweather Novelty would positively *thrive* in a middle school environment!

57

I imagined myself standing before the school board making this great plea, this great case for having a trick shop under our roof.

"Fortuna's number of amateur magicians easily exceeds my dog's flea population!" (Mom says comparisons are very effective in speechmaking.) "Why"—I'd smash my fist into my palm—"there's more sleight of hand around Fortuna any day than there is raising of hands!"

I was getting real eloquent, sitting there in the Pancake House, mentally making this speech while everyone else was busy eating. If I could deliver Merriweather Novelty Co. to the school board—hook, line, and trick sinker—they'd be forced to listen!

"Mom," I said, swinging into action before I lost my nerve, "Steve and I will be late getting home tomorrow after school."

"What's happening?" she said.

I kicked Steve under the table, hard enough so he'd get the message.

"Our committee has some stuff to do."

"Yeah, they're depending on us," Steve rebounded.

"Don't be too late," his mother said, "I don't want the twins staying alone too long."

"Dee could stop over if you need her," Mom volunteered, though Dee was giving her these frantic eyes.

"Thanks, Barbara, but they'll behave themselves until their big brother gets home. You can stay alone for a little while, can't you?"

Now Steve was doing some kicking. I could tell by the pinched look on the twins' little faces and the way they nodded in unison.

11

Pugsley and I had plenty of time on the city bus Monday afternoon to plan our strategy. I would do the talking at Merriweather Novelty. He would back me up.

"You mean," Steve asked, "we tell them they can sell everything at Fortuna but the fake vomit and the doggie-do?"

"Yeah. Mr. Clayton won't go for any of that gross stuff. But that leaves about a thousand other items, you know."

"With Mother's Day coming up," Steve gloated, "they could make a mint on those three-legged panty hose. My mom always asks for a pair of panty hose. Wouldn't she feel lucky to have a pair and a half?"

We chuckled about that for a long time.

The building that housed the novelty company wasn't much to look at, which made me feel better. If they had a real classy place, they'd be less interested in moving to Fortuna (which is "architecturally aesthetic as well as functional," according to the PTA handbills). Merriweather's red-brick building looked as if it had once been a city jail.

Steve and I sort of stood around at first, looking up at these funny little windows that had bars over them.

"You go first," he said. "It's your idea."

"You think I'm scared to?" I didn't budge. "I'm not scared to."

Steve spit on the sidewalk. That's the way he gets up his courage. I tried to, but I didn't have enough saliva.

"C'mon," I said at last, trying to think of Fortuna. I was also remembering my dad, who isn't afraid of anything.

I squared my shoulders and opened the front door of the novelty company with a flourish and a loud bang.

We stopped before we'd taken three steps. The place didn't look like a trick shop at all. There was a railing, such as you'd see at court. Behind that there were three desks— with secretaries, I guess—and a man hidden way back in a separate office. One of the ladies quit typing and looked up.

"May I help you?"

"I'd like to speak to the boss," I said. Then, seeing this look on her face and remembering that women are bosses too, I quickly added, "Maybe *you*'re the boss?"

"Not yet," she said with a smile at the other ladies. "May I have your name, please?"

"I'm Norman Gates. And this is Steve Pugsley."

"And what's the nature of your business?"

Steve looked panic-stricken, but I knew what I was doing.

"We'd like to make a deal with Mr. Merriweather."

"Do you have an appointment?"

I felt my face getting red. How could I have forgotten *that*? In the business world, everyone needs appointments. My father's dental practice would go swirling down the cuspidor without appointments.

She finally got up from her desk. "I'll see if Mr. *Trent* can see you."

Then she left us standing outside the rail. I could tell Steve was a nervous wreck already. At that moment he'd have pleaded guilty to anything to get out of there.

Then she was back, opening the gate, showing us into this inner room behind glass walls. I searched Mr. Trent's face for some sign of friendliness, but he looked stern as an old bulldog. The Cowardly Lion, facing the Wizard of Oz, couldn't have been shaking harder than we were!

"Well," he growled, "do you boys know this is a wholesale house and not a retail outfit?"

He might as well have been talking Chinese.

"Our retail store's over on Fourth and Delaware." He tapped the table with his pencil, like he was counting the seconds he was losing over us. "You want to buy tricks, you go over there. Or out to the Southwood Mall."

"No, sir, we're not here to buy anything," I squeaked.

His eyes went squinty. "What are you here for?"

I'd gone over my speech a dozen times Sunday night, but suddenly I couldn't remember a syllable of it.

"We're here to make a business deal," came Steve's voice. "My friend here wants to tell you about it. Go on, Norman, tell him about it."

Mr. Trent's pencil never stopped tapping, but somehow or other I managed to explain how the board was going to close our school if they couldn't get a tenant to help keep costs down. I told him how terrific it would be if he'd expand his business by putting a trick shop in at Fortuna.

"Merriweather's a household name at our school," I finished after a minute. "You couldn't go wrong, sir."

That compliment must have softened him up. His bulldog jowls started to jiggle and his eyes lost that predator look. Even his pencil stopped tapping.

"Now, I do appreciate you boys thinking of us, but our business is manufacturing. We make the tricks and novelties

61

here, we let other folks sell 'em. But tell me, what's so popular out there at your school that you know about Merriweather?"

I looked at Steve. I didn't want to mention the doggie-do or the plastic vomit. "Snapping gum," I said quickly.

Mr. Trent gave me a blank look.

"You know—" I explained, "it gives your finger a smack when you pull it out of the package."

"Oh, *that*. It's made by our competitor."

I shrank a couple of sizes.

"Mostly what we see around school is disappearing ink," Steve covered for me again. *Disappearing* was exactly what I had in mind right then.

"Sorry I can't help you," Mr. Trent said next, kind of waving us out of his presence as if we were a couple of fakes ourselves, "—but Irene will give you a tour of the place since you've come so far."

We backed away, saying "thank you" and "it's been nice to meet you." I smashed into a potted plant and Steve nearly knocked over a hatrack by the door. It was awful!

Irene, the young secretary who had let us in, was about ten times friendlier, though she trotted us through the back shop in about five minutes.

The mask room was a real tunnel of horrors, with so many twisted and ugly faces you wouldn't believe it. I figured they must have used Mr. Trent as their model.

Irene closed the door on the next area before we got so much as a glimpse inside. "That's X-rated stuff," she explained.

"Like what?" Steve asked before I could poke him.

"Like none of your business," she answered.

Next, Irene showed us the chorus line of three-legged

panty hose. The lady assembling and boxing them hardly looked up from her work, a further hint of how welcome we were. Or maybe she was embarrassed, too, to have so many ladies' legs in the air.

It was the table piled high with hundreds of plucked rubber chickens that interested Steve most. He couldn't resist squeezing the poultry as we went by.

"Poof!" Out shot this stream of talcum powder that landed right on Irene's navy blue skirt.

"Excuse *me*!" Steve croaked.

Irene merely chuckled. "Forget it! Everyone has to squeeze the chickens. It's like the Charmin tissue, you know?" All the time she was talking, she was furiously brushing off her skirt.

Irene got back at Steve when we reached the creams and lotions display.

"Put a little of this in your palm," she said, handing him a can of shaving stuff with a cut lime on the label. "It has the best smell . . . go ahead, try it . . . it's an aerosol."

Steve pressed the button on top. Quickly his hand filled with shaving cream.

"Hey"—he jerked back—"hey!" The foam kept coming, piling up in his palm. I cupped my hands under his. The stuff wouldn't stop—ribbons and ribbons of it, squirting every which way!

"Take it!" Steve shouted at Irene, "it's stuck!"

Then we realized. We'd been tricked.

Irene was having a big old time watching us jump around after the plastic goo that was now draped all over us and our arms.

"Oh my!" she said at last, trying to catch her breath. "I'm the world's worst. I can't pass up the Lucky Lime Shaving Cream. I never can!"

We pulled the goopy ropes off each other, Steve all the time carrying on about how scared he was when the shaving cream wouldn't stop pouring out. We both felt kind of silly.

"I'm sorry, Steve," Irene said as she finished cleaning us up. "I just couldn't help myself."

"So long as you're having fun—" Steve muttered.

The look he gave me had daggers in it—real ones, not the plastic imitations.

But there was more to come.

At the end of the tour we returned to the front office along a narrow, dimly lit hallway. Irene first, Steve next, me bringing up the rear. We'd almost reached the door at the end when "Bigfoot" stepped out of a side hallway and grabbed Steve. You should have heard the shrieks!

Irene cracked up. So did I, but Steve was fighting mad. I actually thought it was funny, especially after I realized who was in the costume, but Steve almost took a poke at Mr. Trent. I couldn't blame Mr. Trent for haw-hawing his head off, even if it was at our expense. Steve had jumped a good foot in the air!

Exactly eighteen minutes after walking into Merriweather Novelty Co. we were out on the street again, slightly dazed from it all. We could still hear them laughing inside the building as we walked away.

Although I was grinning hard myself, Steve had turned a deep shade of red. I was about to point out to him the appropriateness of the Bigfoot disguise. It was like Mr. Trent himself, who was as scary to look at as anyone you'd ever meet, but who was just another practical joker inside. But I never got around to saying it. The scowl on Steve's face stopped me.

"Cripes!" he said, spitting viciously. "Don't ever ask me to do nothing like *that* again!"

I swallowed my grin. Steve was in no mood for comparisons.

I zipped up my parka, hurrying to keep up with him. Clearly he was embarrassed. I guess maybe he'd had his feelings hurt. Who liked being the butt end of a joke, anyway?

"I hate you, Gates!" he burst out suddenly in very plain language. "Next time you want to play sucker, you do it by yourself, you hear?"

I sobered up fast after he said that. What was there to laugh about, anyhow?

By the time we'd walked two blocks and Steve still wasn't speaking, I started to feel really rotten. Maybe I'd been wrong. Maybe Norman Middal Gates was well *below* average. A genuine subnormal stumblebum! What made me think I could save a middle school, for crying out loud? I couldn't do *anything* right.

I followed Steve to the downtown bus terminal, kicking my self-esteem along the ground like so much doggie-do. He didn't talk to me all the way home.

12

fi as co—n., a complete, ignominious failure

vi a ble—adj., practicable; workable, as a viable plan

I was in no mood to be expanding my vocabulary. Especially with the two words Mom paired up on the refrigerator that week.

Fiasco. Noun. "Inspired by that awful school board meeting," Mom said.

If she thought their meeting was a fiasco, she should have been along when Steve and I struck out. But as I was saying, I was in no mood for words like *fiasco* or *viable*. I was tired of trying to be a hero. Who did I think I was, anyway, Luke Skywalker? I was just a growing boy.

Mom was tired of heroics too. "I just can't cope" was the way she put it one night after school as she slumped in a chair and asked me to make her a cup of tea.

My answer was television. *Hers* was writing letters to my dad. I didn't know why she bothered. He wouldn't get them until he was out of the Andes, but she didn't seem to care. She just kept on writing him letters.

And I kept watching *Happy Days*.

And Dee kept on talking about this new kid she'd asked to the dance who was shorter than she was.

I didn't call Steve and he didn't call me. The only time he got friendly was in front of Bogucki's Bakery one day.

"Hey, look, Gates," he said, waiting for me to catch up. "They got a special on cookies. Center fills."

"I'm broke," I answered.

That was the end of that. He ran off ahead of me and I didn't try to catch up.

The one bright spot in my days was seeing Lisa in math class. She was speaking to me now if I happened to bump into her. Or if I spoke first. Or if she positively couldn't get out of it.

"What's new, Norman?" she'd asked once, brightening my whole life.

Karen and Sherry came up just then, so I didn't get a chance to tell her, but at least she'd asked.

We went along that way until the end of April, swapping discouragements. When Mom wasn't talking on the phone with Mildred Fensley (who was still working on that dumb idea of getting a branch library in Fortuna), she was either grading papers or nagging me about my room. Twice, Dee had to fix dinner while Mom went to committee meetings. I just about lost my taste for tomato soup, I can tell you that. So did Animal.

Honest, there were days when I felt just like an orphan. When your sister's off her rocker about some midget, and your mother's off fighting a lost cause, and your father's off doing his own thing, a guy feels about as needed as an extra leg in the panty hose.

Every afternoon I flopped down in front of the tube, Animal beside me, and watched these lucky kids on TV succeed. I went through a box of Twinkies and a jar of peanut butter before Mom even noticed.

Things might have gone on being dismal if it hadn't been for Joe and Mary Conrad, friends of ours who had just returned from Paris. Now, it was *their* fault our dad took off in the first place. As far as I was concerned, they could have stayed away forever, but Mom was overjoyed at their phone call.

Before she hung up, I knew we were having company for dinner that Friday night. Dee would luck out, as usual, since she'd be going to the dance with Shorty. I'd get stuck having to eat with the Conrads, who were fifty years old and who'd forgotten they ever had a childhood.

Worst of all, we always have to shut Animal in my room when they come around. Mrs. Conrad claims she's allergic to dog hairs, so we practically vacuum walls and ceilings before they visit.

"But they're such charming people," my mom says, as if it's worth killing ourselves for an evening of charm. I'd rather have the Pugsleys over any day—spilt milk, fingerprints, unflushed toilets, and all!

Friday night came, as I knew it would, and our living room waited in high-gloss splendor for the Conrads to arrive. Too soon they did.

"Barbara!" Joe gave my mother this big hug at the door. I hardly recognized him. He'd grown a mustache. He also wore a fancy silk scarf at his throat that made him look like a character straight out of a Pink Panther movie.

They all had to kiss and exclaim and carry on. I stayed out of reach.

A little later, helping Mom serve, I carried the tray of drinks and snacks into the living room. Mary Conrad took one of the drinks, dipped a chip in the dilled sour cream, then swooped toward the brocade chair between the sofa and love seat. She didn't even see me—just took what she wanted and swooped away. She might have murmured "darling" at me, but I wasn't sure.

Joe wasn't much better. He patted me on the head and told me I'd really grown in the last six months. (I hadn't.)

Then they were all seated and I put the snacks down on the coffee table.

"Sit here, Norman, we want you to join us," Mom said, making room for me on the sofa.

Mary Conrad, who'd been throwing French phrases around like confetti ever since she walked in, now seemed "oh so interested" in why my dad had gone off and left us. Mom had just started to tell her version when Mrs. Conrad interrupted with a polite gasp: "It was because of us?" She spread her hand over the yards of gold chain wrapped around her neck. "Really?"

"*You,* not *me,*" Mr. Conrad said. "Don't blame me. You were the one who brought the bottle of wine into the dental office."

I remembered.

"What have you been drinking?" That was the first thing Mom said after Dad kissed her that night last October. Then he made Mom sit right down—didn't even take off his coat—and he told her about Joe and Mary Conrad going to Paris. They'd sold their business, rented their house, and were taking off—just like that!

Now, sitting there beside me, Mom started laughing.

"Michael said you'd asked to put a bottle of wine in the toilet tank to keep it cold, right there in his dental office—"

Joe jumped in. "That's exactly what happened. Mary says to him, 'I'm your last patient today, Michael, and you're going to help us celebrate.'"

Then Mary Conrad described how they had used these little paper cups out of the unit and toasted everything French they could think of, ending with the receptionist's ancestors, who were Canadian French.

"And that's where it all began," Mom said, setting down her glass. "Michael decided that you can't put off your dreams forever. You two weren't afraid to interrupt your lives, so to speak . . . and I'd been dying to teach again. You know that, Mary, we used to talk about it all the time—"

"So where is Michael now?" Mrs. Conrad asked. "This very minute."

"Get the atlas, Norman," Mom said, "it's in the family room."

I could hear her telling them how Dad had organized a climbing party among friends he had once spent a summer with in the Colorado Rockies. Two of them had their own businesses now. Brady had climbed with Dad during dental school, until he moved to Washington. There were six of them in all, and they were getting in shape for the Himalayas by climbing peaks in Mexico and South America.

"They're hoping to wind up in Nepal," Mom said as I came back in the room.

Then Mom opened the atlas to the places marked by paper clips and showed them where Dad's party had been and where they were going. If they were on schedule, they might be climbing Cerro Torre about now.

70

"This has been hard on you, hasn't it?" Mrs. Conrad asked my mom. I could see why Mom thought she was charming. She sounded a hundred percent sincere when she tried.

"I worry, of course," Mom answered, "though I try not to. Anyway, my turn comes next year."

I looked up. *Next year? Mom . . . going away next year?*

"What do you mean?" I blurted out.

"It's been hardest on Norman here," Mom said, tousling my hair.

"Where are you going next year?" I insisted loudly.

"I'm going back to the university, Normie. I'll be taking classes to recertify for teaching."

"More tomato soup!" I groaned, trying to be funny now that I'd started breathing again.

"Dad will be here. You say he's a better cook than I am, anyway." She stood to pass the chips and dip.

"So what's all the ruckus about Fortuna?" Mary asked, scooping into the sour cream again.

That, I decided, was a good time for me to slip into the family room and turn on the TV. Low, so I could think. Suddenly I had a lot to think about. Mom really did believe Dad was coming back. He'd convinced her. Totally convinced her. Didn't she remember the fight? How could she forget what he'd said?

I turned on *Wall Street Week in Review*, something that would impress the heck out of the Conrads if they walked in, then stretched out on the sofa and pushed my face into a pillow.

"A man gets trapped . . ." I heard Dad's voice again, as plain as the night they thought I was upstairs asleep. They had just come home from a movie. They'd been arguing in the car, I could tell.

71

"A man gets trapped in his job and can't get out, no matter what."

I heard them hang up their coats. Then they'd gone into the family room. I could still hear them talking through the wall between us.

"Some mornings," my dad said, "I'd like to go right on past that office—right on by, Barbara. I'd like to take off and never come back."

"Michael, you need this trip, don't you see? You'll start resenting us for holding you back! Don't you think I can keep us going while you're away? Don't you have any confidence in *me*?"

"Look, Barbara, you've never had the full responsibility—monthly payments, the cars to take care of, the IRS breathing down your neck—and don't forget there are four mouths to feed—"

"Five! There's Animal, and he has a big mouth."

Things went downhill after Mom made that crack. Pretty soon they were screaming, slamming doors. Mom was crying. I was in the downstairs bathroom in the dark, sitting on the john because ours upstairs had overflowed. That's when I discovered bathrooms were a good place to cry.

Mom and Dad never knew I was there. They never even knew I was out of bed. They were so mad at each other they weren't thinking about Dee and me.

"Why *can't* I go back to work?" Mom kept saying. "Is your macho ego offended if I work, too?"

"Don't insult me, Barbara!"

I stuck toilet paper in my ears.

When I crept back upstairs after everything grew quiet, I could see Mom wrapped up in a blanket on the sofa. It had come to that.

The next month or two I walked around scared most of the time. I knew my dad wouldn't be with us much longer. However, when they finally broke the news, I was better prepared than Dee. She swallowed it all. As far as she was concerned, everything would be old times again in a few months.

I wondered, lying there on the sofa, if *she* knew Mom was going to the university next year. I wondered if I was the only one in the whole world they hadn't bothered to tell. I tried to sort it out in my head. If Mom wasn't teaching and Dad didn't come back, who'd make the money for us to live on? Maybe we'd have to move away—to some little two-room apartment. I'd never see Lisa, or Steve, or any of the kids at school.

I guess it was then I quit sniveling and raised my head out of the pillow. The program on TV had changed. A symphony orchestra was playing now and the tympani player looked like he was slipping a disc.

"Come to dinner, Norman," Mom called from the other room in this cheerful voice, "and leave on the Overture, I love it."

Mom was being braver than any ten dads! I couldn't let her down. I had to grow up and take some responsibility on my own narrow shoulders. Maybe Dad *was* coming back, if Mom was so convinced . . . but then again, maybe he wasn't. And in that case, Mom would need a man around the house.

13

It was Adelsack who got me thinking again about the fate of our poor middle school.

"The media are ignoring Fortuna," she said one day, having a tantrum right in the middle of her fudge demonstration. "And that's the kiss of death."

Cecil Underwood had started it. "The school's going down the tube," he'd remarked as Adelsack laid out her ingredients. "What good did it do to raise all that money?"

Adelsack looked up, her eyes like sharp points of light in her leathery brown face. "No one's taking us seriously. Not the board, the district office, the newspapers—no one! See any coverage on TV? Any big write-ups in the paper?" She motioned us to gather around the demonstration table with its built-in stove top. "Come in close, now. Melting marshmallows can be very tricky."

"Why is it called 'Never Fail' if it's so tricky?" Cecil asked, trying to change the subject once he saw how riled she was.

" 'Never Fail' means it won't be runny after it cools," she said, "but 'tricky' means it's easy to burn."

I doubted if the Underwoods ever burned anything at their house. I had a quick thought about inviting Cecil over some night when Dee was cooking, to broaden his experience.

Now Adelsack was stirring in the chocolate chips. Thirteen male bodies pressed closer for the first rich whiffs curling up and over the edge of the pan. Making Bachelor Fudge was the highlight of the class, and the only reason—Steve said—he'd signed up for it.

Adelsack gave the candy a good beating as she got back on the subject of Fortuna. "Anyone see that letter to the editor yesterday?"

"My mom read it to us at breakfast," I volunteered.

"What'd you think of it, Norman? Tell the boys what it said."

"Well"—I thought for a minute—"it said the district spent more money putting sod in at Eastmont last year than what they *lost* keeping Fortuna open."

"And what happened to that twenty-five thousand dollars' worth of sod and landscaping?"

"The sod didn't take. I guess the grass died because the sprinkler heads didn't get installed fast enough."

"Exactly! And the writer of that letter asked 'What are we paying taxes for? Education or grass transplants? Where are our priorities?' "

She handed the pan around so all of us could see how creamy and shiny the fudge looked.

"Set the timer for five minutes, Greg. Now notice, we turn this burner to low. L-O-W, got it? Repeat after me, L-O-W."

"L-O-W," we said in unison.

"Cecil, you stir for a while. Keep scraping the bottom so it doesn't stick. See anything else in the paper about Fortuna?" she asked, taking a pan out of the cupboard behind her.

"My mom clips everything," Steve said.

"And how many articles has she clipped?"

"One little teeny one."

"Bingo!" From an impressive distance, using a hook shot, Adelsack chucked a square of margarine into the pan. Somebody cheered.

"If your hands are still clean," she said to Steve, "rub that around. Cover the bottom good, you hear?"

She wasn't through with her lecture yet. "So what's going to move that school board to change their minds? We can't just sit around and pray, now, can we? We need to draw some attention to ourselves. Make a noise!"

"That's what my dad says," Dennis Wagner spoke up.

"—and he's right!"

Adelsack sniffed at the pan Cecil was tending, then she straightened up and gave us this serious look. "Timidity is"—she paused to think—"timidity is standing around waiting for those buses to arrive. Sure enough, they'll arrive if everyone expects them to. If I were you kids or your parents, I'd be stirring up more than fudge around here!"

Adelsack didn't know it, but she was stirring me up plenty. She was a hundred percent right about the media not paying attention, but what could anyone do about it? What could I, a mere seventh grader who'd just started using deodorant, do to get the newspapers or the TV interested in Fortuna?

The rest of the day I puzzled over our predicament. Finally, during math class, I had this brilliant idea. It wouldn't have occurred to me, either, except for Lisa, who was wearing a new hot-pink T-shirt. "Today Is My Birthday," it said across her chest. You had to get embarrassingly close to read the message. The letters were microscopic. Even Mr. Henry made a big fuss over Lisa, getting out his magnifying glass and acting silly. Naturally, we all ended up singing "Happy Birthday, dear Leeeesa." I couldn't believe all the attention she was getting because of a few words on a T-shirt.

Then the idea struck me. Flattened me in fact! Rolled me over and sat on my belly. T-shirts, of course! Cheap, easy, movable advertising!

Suddenly I pictured everyone in school wearing yellow T-shirts with dark blue letters, every student parading a message in school colors. I visualized this sea of uniformed students surging out of the school, moving toward the TV cameraman. I could see Mr. Clayton himself being interviewed: "Can you tell us what's happening here at Fortuna, sir?"

I could hardly breathe, I was so excited. I wanted to tell Steve, but he was still burned from our fiasco at Merriweather Novelty Co. This caper I'd have to pull off myself. But I wasn't worried. The old confidence surged through me. If there was ever a plan you could call viable (adjective, meaning practicable, workable), this was it!

I chuckled, hunched there over this math test I was taking on the division and multiplication of fractions. I knew one teacher who'd wear a T-shirt along with the kids, and it wasn't Mr. Henry!

Five days later a delivery truck deposited three big boxes on our doorstep. There were a hundred Smalls, eighty Mediums, twenty Larges. Every single one had "Fortuna Forever" emblazoned across the front in navy blue script.

I made sure I was home early to sign for them.

Norman Gates, I wrote beside the X where the delivery man told me to, my fingers trembling only slightly.

I knew what I'd done was a bold move, but Adelsack

said we'd get exactly what we deserved if we sat around on our buns. Lucky for me the Shirt Shack had let me charge all two hundred T-shirts to Mom's VISA card number. "Has this been authorized?" was all the man asked me on the phone. I didn't know exactly what he meant, so I explained I was ordering them for Fortuna Middle School for a fund drive. That made it okay with him.

What I hadn't counted on was having my mother go to pieces when she saw what I'd done.

"*Norman Middal Gates!*" she screeched, whipping her calculator out of the desk, "do you know what kind of money we're talking about here?"

"A thousand dollars even," I answered calmly. "They're five bucks apiece. A dollar off, the man said, because of volume, and schools don't have to pay tax."

14

Myself, I wasn't worried. Even though Mom threatened to exchange me for a foster child, I knew Operation T-shirt would succeed. Why, within a matter of minutes I'd made three sales—to Dee, Mom, and me. That left only 197 bright yellow Fortuna Forever T-shirts on the dining-room table for all those other people who'd want them. I began wondering if I'd ordered enough.

Dee, suddenly on my side, showed me how to make order pads for people who couldn't pay on the spot. She knew a lot about selling. She was once the best cookie-pusher in her Girl Scout troop. She also promised she'd get all her friends to buy T-shirts.

"I know Jennifer will want one," she said after Mom had gone upstairs to lie down. "In fact, I'll help you sell these if you want me to."

I looked at her suspiciously. "How come?"

"Well, if you *don't* want me to—"

"I just wonder why you're being so nice, that's all."

"Norman, don't be childish. These T-shirts could become a status symbol." She fingered them, held various ones up in the air, folded them again. "Don't you just *love* the smell of new clothes?"

She'd missed the whole point. But Normal Norman was not one to turn down an offer of assistance. Quickly, I recovered my manners.

"I'd be deeply honored," I said, "to have you help me."

I got a fishy look from her next. "You're just lucky Dad wasn't home. He'd make you take them back."

"I wish he was home," I said with a sigh. "Do you think . . . I mean, do you think Dad's really coming home after Nepal?"

"Of course he is. Where else would he go?"

"Steve's dad never came back."

"Steve's dad! What's he got to do with anything?"

"He said he was coming back, too. Went to Mexico for their quickie divorce and—poof!—disappeared into thin air. Steve can't even remember him."

"Norman! Why would Dad do that? You get the dumbest ideas sometimes."

I shrugged and stapled an order pad together.

By that time Dee's eye had fallen on the unused telephone, at which point Dad and I both lost out.

"Why don't you go in the other room?" she said with her usual tact. "I need to call Jennifer. Maybe she can come over and try on T-shirts with me."

I swear, my sister Delilah wouldn't notice if our family was busting up. Someone would have to point it out to her. She didn't care about Fortuna, either, or getting the media interested in the school's fate. All she cared about was STATUS. The shirts could have carried any message ("Ima Drip," "Hog Waller"), but if everyone was going to be wearing them, Dee would have to be first.

I went out into the garage to do some pull-ups on Dad's

chinning bar. Why did I have to worry so much about everything? I had definitely become a better-than-average worrier since February. *Be glad she wants to help,* I told myself. *Out blitzing the neighborhood, you'll need all the help you can get, sincere or otherwise.*

Mom let us out of our usual chores that Saturday so we could begin selling right after breakfast. It was a warm spring day, so Dee, Jennifer, and I all wore the shirts we were selling. We looked pretty terrific, like a regular sales force, if I do say so myself.

"Good luck!" we told each other before we split up. They headed south and I headed north toward Lisa's.

I had wanted to ask Steve to help, but Mom said he wouldn't look too "savory" at nine on a Saturday morning.

She was right. I went to his place first. I wanted to try out my sales pitch on someone I knew before assailing the general public. Besides, with the competency tests coming up, Steve had been lots friendlier at school, so I knew we were gradually making up.

I shouldn't have bothered. The Pugsleys were still in bed. It took four rings to get anyone to answer and then it was Steve's mom, looking really hashed without her makeup.

"Come back later," she whispered hoarsely from behind the door, "Steve's still in the sack."

I decided to catch Lisa on my way back home. I'd die if I got *her* out of bed.

All in all I woke up at least seven families, was kept from one door by a big Siamese cat, and was told to "beat it" by old Mr. Crampton, who hadn't softened one bit since the day we did the survey. By noon I had sold exactly five

T-shirts. Karen bought one, Lisa's mother bought one for Lisa. ("She's having a piano lesson now, Norman.") Steve and Mrs. Pugsley ordered two mediums, to be delivered on Glenna's payday. The milkman said he'd take a large if I'd leave it in the milkbox on Tuesday.

Dee and Jennifer hadn't done much better. They had sold eight, including the one Jennifer bought and wore.

"Everyone thinks it's a marvelous idea," Jennifer said dejectedly, "but nobody buys."

Then Dee had to mimic this one prissy lady who had sounded so insulted: "I never order magazine subscriptions at the door!" She hadn't even asked what they were selling.

The girls fell into a fit of giggling over that, then stumbled off to Dee's room.

Meanwhile, I was doing some mental arithmetic. Eight plus five plus three equals sixteen. Two hundred, take away sixteen. I slumped onto a stool at the kitchen counter and put my head down on my arms. I might have to get a job walking dogs, after all.

Mom, however, was all lovey-dovey and optimistic. A total schizo, she was controlled by her *sweet* personality today.

"You'll sell them at school, Normie," she said, "just be patient. I know kids. They'll all want one when they see you and your friends wearing them around."

I propped my head up with my hand and watched her grill the cheese sandwiches, wondering why such a good cook would want to take classes at the university. She set out the pickles, a basket of chips, drinks for all of us, including Jennifer.

"I'm sorry I flew into you last night," she apologized, "but

82

if you ever use my VISA number again, I'll cut off both your ears."

I knew she didn't mean *that,* but I'd learned my lesson. She'd made me sign an IOU for every penny of the thousand dollars plus any interest that was tacked on.

She handed me a sandwich. "I guess I shouldn't discourage you. You really do have the makings of an entrepreneur."

"What's *that?*" I asked.

"An entrepreneur's a businessman. Someone who takes the risks and responsibilities for a business." She laughed softly. "Grandpa Middal calls them 'wheeler-dealers' sometimes."

I didn't like the sound of it, but already I could see Monday's word captured under the strawberry magnet. I'd never learn to pronounce it, let alone use it!

15

The bad news came home with my mom the next Monday night. Things had looked good at first. Mildred Fensley's committee had finally interested the public library in opening a branch at Fortuna Middle School. The next step was convincing the school board that it would work.

Armed with a hundred reasons why a "housed" library would serve the neighborhood better than the rickety old bookmobile, and well supplied with figures proving that shared usage would cut costs, Mom left for the meeting in high spirits. She just knew the school board couldn't turn down such a "viable alternative," as she liked to call it.

Wrong again.

My mother was *so* furious when she returned home! I knew it the instant I heard the door slam. When I heard the click of her heels across the entryway, I tossed my copy of *Mad* aside and rushed out to meet her.

"Those incompetent, waffle-brained—" she sputtered, waving a fistful of papers in the air. "These objections were run off a week ago! They'd made up their minds before they ever *heard* our presentation. Not only that, Norman, they adjourned early so the president of the board could catch his plane to Hawaii! Oh, wow, big deal! Don't let a little thing like a middle school stand in the way of your trans-oceanic cocktails!"

Boy, was she burned! I didn't say a word. I could tell she was yelling to keep from crying.

She crumpled the papers, chucked them onto the dining-room table, and headed for her bedroom. Once she got on the extension with Glenna, I smoothed out the pages to read them with my own eyes.

"Incompatible Objectives" headed the list and was followed by a long explanation of what that meant. "Duplication of Services" brought on another paragraph. "Additional Custodial Requirements," likewise. It went on and on for four pages, in language mostly above my head.

I'd known all along that the idea of a library wouldn't go over, but this was not the time to say so. What I was feeling was sick to my stomach. It isn't easy to stand by and see your mom fail time after time.

I vowed then to double my efforts on the T-shirts. The PTA was finished, that was plain, but there was no way I'd give up. Normal Norman might be your average-looking middle-sized middle school kid, but he was born with a giant's share of determination. (Or *tenacity*, if you prefer the fancy word to the plain the way my mother does.)

I got as far as Thursday that week before running into trouble. I'd been selling T-shirts like crazy. Already the halls were livening with color. Yellow shirts, like daffodils in spring, were cropping up everywhere. Then Miss Griffin turned me in. I was pretty sure she was the one.

"Not in my class, Norman!" she said when she caught Dennis Wagner slipping me a five-dollar bill during English.

"Don't you know the district office has issued a directive?" she asked sharply.

I didn't know what she was talking about, but very shortly I found out.

"Norman Gates," blared the intercom during Singles' Survival. "Please come to the office. Norman Gates, to the office, please." (I love it when they repeat your name that way. It sort of doubles your pleasure, if you get what I mean.)

It was the Big C himself who wanted to see me, so I knew it was serious.

"Sit down, Norman," Mr. Clayton said after we shook hands. He got right to the point. "I can't allow you to sell one more T-shirt on school property."

I gulped. "I've only sold twenty-nine here at school, sir."

"I know your intentions are the best," he said, rocking back in his chair and folding his hands over his vest. "You've really thrown yourself into the fight, though we all seem to have lost at this point." Then he smiled. "I'd be out peddling Fortuna Forevers myself if I didn't care about having a job next year, but the school board hires me and they're finding the community's opposition to closure embarrassing."

When he sat forward, his voice turned confidential. "The truth is, Norman, they're threatening to string me up if any more promotions are conducted here on school property."

"What am I going to do with a hundred and fifty-five T-shirts?" I groaned. "Even old Methuselah couldn't wear out that many!"

Mr. Clayton merely shook his head and looked sad. Finally, he stood up.

"I do appreciate your loyalty to the school. Oh, by the

way . . . a Mr. Trent—Merriweather Novelty Company—called a while back. Said he was very much impressed by how enterprising some of our students are. Know anything about that?"

"Yes, sir," I gulped again.

He threw back his head and laughed. "You're all right, Norman!"

Then he walked me to the door of his office.

"I don't suppose the powers-that-be could stop you from selling T-shirts in your own driveway . . . or from conducting a telephone solicitation . . ." He spread his hands. "I'd like to have one myself, but I couldn't wear it." (Mrs. Adelsack was wearing *hers*. Under a blazer, to be sure, but she'd been flashing it around all week.)

"Actually," Mr. Clayton whispered, getting right down to my level, "I hope you sell them *all*. But don't tell anyone I said so."

Suddenly we were exchanging grins. And just as suddenly my spirits lifted. *He* wanted to save the school as much as I did! Maybe more! But he was the principal. His hands were tied, as they say. Well, mine for sure weren't!

I headed on down the hall, noticing an extra springiness in the soles of my Nikes.

Back in home ec class, I asked Mrs. Adelsack if I could have an appointment with her after school. (I'd learned to ask for appointments.)

"You betcha," she said. She slid half of Cecil's fluffy omelet onto a plate for me to taste. "You got problems?"

"Yeah, my Clearasil's not working," I said so everyone could hear.

*　*　*

87

That afterschool conference was the turning point. It's easy to put your finger on things like that when you're looking back at them. If Adelsack had been going to the hairdresser's that day or grading tests or going to one of her dreaded faculty meetings, I'm pretty sure the outcome at Fortuna would have been different.

Funny how often history hinges on chance. Sitting there in Mr. Clayton's office, a little old unformed idea had flashed across my mind. A mere tickle of inspiration. But I acted on it. I guess that's what people do when they get desperate.

Adelsack stayed there at school with me for two hours. Once she had me go to the phone to report to my mom, but the rest of the time her IN CONFERENCE sign was outside on the door so that no one—*but no one*—bothered us. She even turned away the janitor, who was hanging around waiting to do her room.

"I'll sweep up myself," she told him. "Go on home to dinner."

She winked at me after saying that. No one spoke to old Mr. Trotter that way.

That Thursday I left school with a list in my pocket and those same old trumpet sounds in my ears. The fact that I still owed my mom $775 didn't bother me anymore. Even the anxiety of not hearing from my dad for weeks lost some of its hold on me. What I was about to do filled my entire cranial cavity.

I was glad I didn't have to do it alone.

16

I spent the next Saturday morning getting my gear together and crossing items off the list Adelsack and I had made. At the last minute I cleaned my room so Mom wouldn't have reason to get on me. After everything else was done, I dialed Pugsley's number.

"Meet me at Bogucki's," I told Steve on the phone, making my voice sound mysterious. "Cinnamon rolls come out of the oven at two. I'm going to need an alibi tonight and you're *it*." I knew he'd be there.

The rest of Plan A (for Adelsack) I explained to him on the school grounds, where we took our hot rolls and two Cokes. There was no chance of being overheard there on the grass.

Steve didn't interrupt me once while I explained Mission Impossible to him. When I finished, he gave me one long, unbelieving look and keeled over backward.

"Gates!" he moaned, covering his face. "I don't know you. I never did!"

I couldn't help laughing. "You got to help me, Steve, this is real important."

Finally his color returned to normal and he straightened up. I could hear him gritting his teeth.

"Okay," he said. "So I call your house and ask you to sleep over at my place. Is that all? What if your mom says no?"

"She'll let me. She's been depressed. She'll be glad to get me out of the house." Then I thought of something else. "Hey, what's *your* mom doing tonight? We can't have any foul-ups—"

"What's she ever doing on a Saturday night?"

"Is she going on a date?"

Steve nodded, helping himself to a third cinnamon roll. "Every Saturday night I tend the twins. I'll be doing that when I'm thirty."

I did some fast arithmetic. "Yeah, but by then they'll be—"

"Shut up! You always have to connerdict me?"

"Sor-*ry!*"

"Hey, guess what?" He crushed his can with one hand, splatting me with Coke. "I really like this new guy she's going with."

"Yeah?"

"He's a ham radio operator. He takes me fishing all the time and once we played Asteroids at the Fun Gallery for two straight hours."

"No kidding? How come you haven't told me?"

"I don't know. Him and me . . . we've been busy doing stuff. He let me drive his van one day. Eddie's teaching me Morse code, too, in case I ever need it. He says you never know when you're gonna lose your voice."

I was impressed.

"Da-da-te-dah, da-te-da-da-daaaah—" he sent a telegram on my arm.

I was happy for Steve. A little jealous, but happy. He'd

been fatherless a lot longer than I had. Normally I'd have let him carry on, but I had to get back to my own plans.

"Say, Pugsley, do you still have that pup tent?"

"Yeah, why?"

"Can you set it up in the backyard before your mom leaves? You know, so she'll figure we're asleep out there when she gets home?" I handed him my empty can to flatten.

Suddenly he swung around to face me, his eyes lighting up. "Hey, I'll make a dummy out of some blankets and stuff. Like guys do when they escape from prison. You're the dummy, get it?"

"Steve, you're brilliant!"

"And I'll play my transistor radio out there. Mom won't suspect a thing!" Steve wadded up the empty sack and tossed it overhead. "Whoooeee! Am I glad you're doing this and not me!"

"You think I'm crazy, don't you?"

"Gates, I always thought you had a screw loose, especially after Merriweather."

Talking about Merriweather Novelty, we both fell apart.

"Remember how that guy grabbed me?" Steve howled. Pretty soon we were rolling around on the grass like old times, sillier than a couple of girls.

When we got back home, we slapped hands and promised we weren't going to get mad at each other again. Then he took off.

After dinner, when everything was arranged and innocent-looking, I hoisted my backpack and told Mom and Dee to have fun without me.

"Now listen. Don't you and Steve run around the neighborhood after dark," Mom said pointedly, "just because you're sleeping outside."

"Steve's tending, remember? His mother would kill us if we did that."

Mom kissed me good-bye. "Be sure to thank Glenna for breakfast tomorrow morning."

"If I get any . . ." I muttered.

Mom laughed. It was a good sound to leave on. I hadn't heard my mother laugh for five whole days.

17

I walked around behind the school where Mrs. Adelsack said she'd park by the shop building. She was there, all right, in her battered blue Volks, but she had company. Mr. Trotter, the janitor, was leaning on the car window talking to her. What was *he* doing at school? I checked my watch. It was almost seven, and Saturday night besides.

I slowed, wondering if I should turn around and come back after he left. But wearing a loaded backpack made me pretty conspicuous. Adelsack had already seen me. She motioned me to come ahead, then got out of the car herself.

"Norman, you know Mr. Trotter," she said, as if I hadn't seen him every school day of my life.

I smiled, but as usual his expression was set in cement.

"Decided we needed some technical assistance," Adelsack explained, wrinkles forming around her eyes.

Trotter didn't say a word, just walked away, unhooking his jangly keys from his belt as he went.

Mrs. Adelsack opened her trunk, handed me a boxful of stuff, then took out a roll of butcher paper, a collapsible five-gallon container, and a rucksack. We followed Mr. Trotter.

"I probably should read you your rights," she said, holding open the shop door so I could duck through.

I said, "Don't worry about me," but I was glad she couldn't hear the racket my heart made bouncing off my ribs.

We must have looked funny stumbling along with our burdens, led by this silent, gray-headed old man. I thought of refugees heading for the homeland.

We filed into the auditorium through a stage door, climbed a flight of open metal steps to a catwalk above the stage, and then proceeded a slow 40 feet along that to yet another set of steps. I kept wishing I had Dad's 150 feet of Gold Line rope. What a wonderful place to rappel off!

Finally we stood facing a heavy door that Mr. Trotter had some trouble opening.

"I won't relock this," he said with a rare smile, "case you change your mind about all this foolishness."

"Frank Trotter"—Adelsack pushed out her chin—"when did you ever know me to change my mind?"

A look passed between them. I was beginning to suspect they knew each other better than I thought. The rumor that she sometimes left cookies on the counter for him after school, plus the bossy way she talked to him—the fact that he was here at all!—added up to something.

We were all sort of standing there at the door, hesitating.

"Want that water jug filled?" he asked, grumpy once more.

"Sure, you betcha!" Adelsack handed him the plastic container. "That would be a great help. We have plenty to do before dark."

Then the One-and-Only Adelsack and Normal Norman Gates—kid most likely to recede—stepped out onto the flat gravel roof of Fortuna Middle School and looked around for a place to set up a tent.

"We need to be seen," Adelsack said, favoring a site near the front of the building.

"Perfect!" she exclaimed a minute later.

I slid off my pack, untied the two-man tent, and spread out the ground cloth. Now I was in my element. Dad and I used to have contests to see who could put up the backpacking tent fastest. My best time was eight minutes, established at the boulder field camp below Long's Peak last summer. I came close to matching it that Saturday night. I put on a good enough show to impress Adelsack, anyway, who stood there clucking like a whole symphony of hens.

"Boy oh boy!" she'd say now and again. "Would you look at that?"

We tied the zipper flaps back under the rainfly and rolled out a double mat inside. I thought of my dad, how he'd be sleeping under a similar sky tonight. I imagined myself on top of Mount Marmolejo or Cerro Plomo where Dad might be, and somehow the idea put starch in my spine. I smiled across the tent at Adelsack.

"Thanks for doing this with me," I managed.

"No sweat."

"I hope you don't get in trouble."

"Me? Not a chance. The district's been begging me to supervise Title IX changes in all the home ec departments. They want me over the whole kit and kaboodle next year."

"You mean you won't be teaching anymore?"

"Well—*they* want to promote me. Tell you the truth, Norman, I've never been in such a good position to pull off a stunt like this. I bet you four chicken gizzards anyone else would be fired for what I'm doing!"

I marveled as we tied into some vents for protection against wind. Why would Adelsack be so willing to stick out her neck for Fortuna when she could be a big-time supervisor? I had to ask her.

"Well," she said, hands on hips, elbows up in the grasshopper position, "I believe in Fortuna, simple as that. This school is unique. Look at the small classes here, the good teachers. This school is the heart of the neighborhood, lots of parents participating in activities. Yessir, Fortuna and quality education are synonymous, in my opinion."

She paused then and sat down on her rucksack. I had one more corner to tie in.

"I guess Fortuna's become my family, Norman. Maybe I just can't face another empty nest."

"Did you have some kids of your own?"

"Oh, yes, a boy and a girl. But they took wing soon after my husband died. They both attended city schools, but I can tell you, the education there can't compare to what you kids get at Fortuna. And overcrowding Roy and Clearfield isn't the answer at all. Any nincompoop can see that."

I agreed.

"Fortuna's cause is bigger than you and me, Norman. And *we* know it! When the board turned down that library proposal—which made perfectly good sense—I started looking around for some extreme measure myself. I'm the one should be thanking you."

I didn't know what to say to that. It wasn't a hundred percent true. My ideas and hers came together like a spark and combustible twigs. But for all we knew that night, we might not get more going than smoke and smolder.

It was almost dark by the time we got our supplies arranged on the back side of the tent. So far the only ones who had noticed us were two little kids bicycling around the parking lot. They stopped once, stared, waved, went on making swoops and circles. Ho-hum! So what if there's an orange backpacking tent on top of the school?

"That's what TV does to kids," Adelsack muttered, *"nothing's* incredible anymore!"

Lights were popping on in the houses facing the grounds. We stood at the front edge of the roof, two stories up, trying to identify familiar landmarks downhill from us. The 7-Eleven stood out, as did Slim's Gas and Go. Once I thought I could see Steve's place, but Lisa's house and mine were covered by trees that had just leafed out. To the north, lights were beginning to outline the crazy way the city had grown.

Pretty soon I felt like pulling on a sweat shirt.

Adelsack dug in her rucksack and brought out what she called her original Macgregor parka (original in 1950). After adding a striped cap, she did a few jumping jacks to warm up.

"If it gets too cold before bedtime, we'll go inside and jog around," she said, eyes twinkling.

I grinned, picturing the two of us running through the empty halls, our joggers echoing in tandem.

After it was too dark to play any more poker, we settled on having a little nightcap, as Adelsack called it.

"Ever seen such a feast?" she asked as she laid out our snack on the pebbly roof. She poured steaming lemonade from a thermos into Styrofoam cups. My saliva surged.

"Are you prepared to be a laughingstock next week in school, Norman? We don't know how this will turn out."

"I been bracing myself," I said, and took a handful of cheddar curd.

She settled down beside me on her rucksack and we sipped

at our hot drinks. The sour taste zinged into my nose and set my head tingling. I thought of my dad, sipping hot drinks in high places, and felt closer to him than I had in a long time. I was taking risks, too. Of another kind.

I also thought about Steve. I'd never be able to tell him afterward how much fun I was having. He said he'd have wall-to-wall nightmares if he had to sleep with Adelsack.

Finally, it was time.

We made a trip inside to the johns first, carrying flashlights and toothbrushes. Back again, we arranged our sleeping bags so we were half in, half out of the tent. The night was so calm and beautiful we didn't want to miss any of it.

For the longest time we didn't talk, we just lay there on our backs and stared at the sky.

"Makes you feel puny, doesn't it?" my teacher said at last. "Really."

"Guess we are puny . . . in relation to all the rest," she added.

"My dad says the universe goes on beyond man's imagination. How do you *imagine* beyond your imagination? That's what puzzles me."

Adelsack chuckled softly. "He sounds like a regular philosopher. What did he think about this overnight of yours?"

"Oh, he's not home. He's climbing mountains down in Chile."

"You don't say!" Adelsack turned toward me and raised up on one elbow. "Not by himself, I hope."

I told her about my dad, then, and she acted as if she'd never heard anything so interesting.

"What do you know!" she said when I finished. "You Gates men tackle the big ones, don't you?"

Her saying it made me glow in the dark.

"When's he due home, Norman?"

I hesitated. "*Mom* thinks he'll be back in June."

"But you don't?"

I stared hard at the North Star overhead. "I been worried about it."

"You miss him a lot, I guess."

I nodded. I also blinked away the film that was bothering my eyes. "I sometimes worry that he won't come back," I confessed.

"You think your father might be killed?"

Killed! The word sliced into me like a knife. How could she say that? How could she just say that word? I never said it, even to myself—I couldn't! Mom didn't say it, either. It wasn't—it wasn't even a word in our vocabulary!

"Is that what worries you?" Adelsack asked again.

I couldn't answer. I'd been telling myself that Dad was running away, taking off, the way Steve's old man did when his family got in the way of his fun. I'd been preparing myself to live without a father. Was it the idea of *death* that really had me scared? Adelsack's words—*You think your father might be killed?*—were a hard-knuckled fist in the face. My mom *had* been hiding something from me, but it wasn't what I'd thought. We'd been hiding fear from each other—all of us. Hideous, shivering *fear!*

I sat up straight, clutching at the rainfly of the tent. "Yeah, that's what scares me," I said in a voice too loud. "I may never see him again!"

Adelsack knew. I could tell by the current passing between us. Two seconds later I was crying on her shoulder like a great big baby and I couldn't stop.

"Norman," she comforted me, "poor Norman."

Yes, he might be killed, I forced myself to admit it, sobbing still. *And he might never come back and I might end up like Steve!*

"You take my word for it, kid"—Adelsack patted me as I pulled away—"your daddy's coming home. He's a skilled climber, you said so yourself. He'll be back. You and your old man will be so proud of each other you'll be popping buttons all over the place."

I wiped my face on the sleeve of my sweat shirt. "We haven't heard from him for a long time now," I said, suddenly very embarrassed.

"Yeah? Well, that's a long way away for carrier pigeons. Those mountains in Chile are primitive as hell."

Adelsack's cuss word made me smile in spite of myself. I sniffled and lay back down again.

"It takes a lot of trust on your part to let your dad go off that way, Norman. He must have trusted you, too. Figured you were old enough—tough enough—to leave for a while.

"You've been under a lot of strain," she went on talking, "both your worlds going belly-up at the same time. I think you're handling the situation at your end with courage and imagination, that's what *I* think."

She was right about one thing. My dad had trusted me. But I hadn't trusted him, even a little bit. I'd been mad at him for almost four long months, more willing to have him be a deserter—and alive!—than admit he might be flown home in a casket.

Why had I lied to myself? Dad wouldn't run off. He never would. He wasn't like Steve's dad at all. *Only way he'd leave us was if he was dead. That's* what I hadn't been able to face. I'd traded one fear for another, one that I could halfway handle.

100

"Know what Shakespeare wrote once?" Adelsack said, plumping her Macgregor original into a more satisfactory pillow. "'Cowards die many times before their deaths; the valiant never taste of death but once.'"

I puzzled it over. "I don't get it," I confessed.

Adelsack grinned up at the sky. "If the dear old bard will forgive me, that means 'most of the things you worry about never come to pass.'"

"Oh." That I understood.

The next thing I knew it was morning and Adelsack was asking me if I planned to sleep all day.

18

I looked at my watch. *Seven o'clock, yikes!*

I flew below to the john, cleaned up, put on my Fortuna T-shirt. By the time I was topside again, Adelsack was wearing hers, too. She also had our butcher-paper banner rolled out on the roof.

"People will see that for a country mile!" she chuckled.

We cut off long strips of vent tape then and positioned the banner so it hung along the edge of the roof, taping it in a dozen places. I read it out loud, heaping on the dramatics: "If *we* can share housing, *anyone* can!"

"Ta da!" Adelsack said, and we did a little stage business.

We also fastened colored pennants along the edge that said things like "Shared Usage Makes Good Cents," "Caring Is Sharing," and "Fortuna's Future Begins Today."

It was while standing around admiring our artwork that we noticed an innocent-looking tennis ball sitting twenty yards or so beyond the tent.

Adelsack's eyes narrowed. "That wasn't there last night, was it?"

I ran over and picked it up. A paper was taped to it with a message in scrawly handwriting: *1:33 A.M. You been spotted! A man on the talk show said a UFO landed on top of Fortuna. Ha ha! Yours truly, Steve.*

"It's from Pugsley!"

Adelsack read the note, beaming the same as me. To think Steve had been there during the night and we hadn't known it!

It gave us both a little surge, so we treated ourselves to some exercise, tossing the ball around. I tried a spinner on her and she fooled me with a behind-the-back pass. When Adelsack missed and it went over the edge, she decided it was time to quit and fix breakfast anyway.

"Where's your little backpacking stove, Norman? I'll whip us up something."

Her "something" turned out to be sausage, eggs, rolls, and juice. I thought I'd died and gone to the Hilton! She even let me have coffee when I told her I preferred that to chocolate.

So there we sat, hunched over our scrambled eggs, feeling really terrific. Below us the Sunday morning neighborhood stretched and yawned. A paper boy pedaled past. A man and woman came jogging through the parking lot; they gave us big smiles and thumbs-up shouts of encouragement. We laughed and waved before they disappeared behind the school.

"I was going to ask you"—I said when I remembered—"how you got the janitor to let us in the building last night."

"Wellll . . ." Adelsack said, "I just asked. We're old friends, Frank and I. We were very serious about each other in high school."

"You . . . *and Mr. Trotter*?" I stopped eating altogether. "But he's such an old grouch!" I said without thinking.

Adelsack stirred her coffee. "Our senior year he cut a very dashing figure, Norman. He was drum major with the band,

103

I played the clarinet. We thought we were made for each other." She chortled to herself.

"What happened to your . . . uh . . . romance?"

"I went to college, he went to work. That's what happened."

We smiled at each other. I could have gone on talking with Adelsack that way forever. I liked having her treat me like an adult, telling me about her personal life and everything. I guess she'd forgotten I was just a punk kid in one of her classes. Or maybe when two people have breakfast on top of the school, they just naturally feel closer.

"Frank Trotter should have retired last year when his missis did," Adelsack said, and forked up the last sausage for me. "But then, what would we have done for a conspirator?"

"You're never going to retire, are you?" I asked.

"Not as long as I'm having fun. This camp-out will set my clock back at least ten years. Can't you see me 'youthening' already?" She pumped up a bicep that was so minuscule I fell over laughing.

Our leisurely breakfast was the last calm before the storm. Our plan, of course, was to draw attention to Fortuna's plight by protesting the school board's latest decision. We didn't know what would happen or when, but we were pretty sure we wouldn't be ignored. What we didn't expect was for the entire Fortuna family to rise up the way they did that day.

By midmorning something suspicious was going on at Dennis Wagner's house, directly across the street from the school parking lot. Cars were lining up. People were milling around. I recognized Dennis. His mom and dad were outside too. "Hang in there!" he yelled once from his driveway.

"Spunky kid," Adelsack said, "what's he up to?"

Doors opened and shut, card tables were set out on the curbing. Two men strung a rope between trees, high up.

"They're gonna hang us!" I kidded Adelsack.

Then a wildly decorated van arrived and parked in the street. The driver got out and handed boxes to Dennis. I caught a flash of color. I stood and walked to the edge of the roof. What were they doing?

Then Dennis began pinning up Fortuna Forever T-shirts along the rope . . . six in all . . . yellow flags, highlighted with fancy blue script. No lie, they were setting up a roadside stand!

"Look, they're going to sell my T-shirts!" I practically shrieked.

Adelsack and I pumped hands, grinning and grinning.

We hardly noticed the van was moving again until it turned into the parking lot and approached the school. We stopped celebrating. It crawled along the marked fire lane, then parked below us in Mr. Clayton's reserved spot.

"Who comes," Adelsack said under her breath, "friend or foe?"

"It's my mom!" I choked.

Sure enough, Barbara Gates was sticking her head out on the passenger side. You can't believe how relieved I was when she started blowing kisses at me. Man, I was so relieved, I wasn't even embarrassed!

Glenna Pugsley was there too, leaning over my mom, trying to see us.

"STAY BACK FROM THE EDGE!" came this booming

male voice. Adelsack jumped a mile. The voice *had* to belong to Glenna's new boyfriend, though Steve never mentioned Eddie had a sound system in his van.

I could see my mother reaching for the mike. "Are you all right?" she asked first off.

"Yeah, we're fine," I called back.

"I don't know if I can stand any more surprises, Norman." Her voice wavered out for the whole world to hear, making me cringe.

I guess she didn't like going public, either, because she got out then and hurried up to the building. I knelt at the edge so we could see each other.

She said, "Next time you get inspired, maybe you could let me in on it, huh?"

I squirmed. Adelsack didn't know I hadn't asked permission. Hurriedly I introduced my teacher and my mom, hoping good manners would make up for what I'd left out.

"Steve's been calling everyone," Mom told us. "He and Dennis have appointed themselves to be your backup squad."

"Where's Steve now?" I asked.

Mrs. Pugsley, who was hanging out of the window, said, "He's still on the phone. Can you believe he's trying to round up the pep band? I've got a crazy feeling, Norman, this school's gonna rise again!"

Good old Glenna! She could revive a petrified log!

"How long do you plan to hold out?" Mom asked. "No, wait"—she threw up her hands—"don't answer that—I'd rather not know!"

Adelsack laughed. "Don't worry about us. This is an exceptional young man I have up here with me."

"Isn't he, though? Keep a good eye on him or he'll sell you the Brooklyn Bridge."

Mom left then, the three of them waving, Eddie wishing us good luck over the PA.

Exceptional. Is that what Adelsack had said? I felt a smug smile coming on, then remembered a guy should be careful when he gets so high up. Altitude sickness can cut you down in a hurry.

After that, everything happened so fast I have a hard time remembering the order of things. My mom got out at the Wagners', I guess to help sell T-shirts. Eddie and Glenna, in the van, started down the street, drumming up business. "Now is the time for all good patrons to come to the aid of their school!" reverberated Eddie's voice through the loud-speakers. "Clyde?" he'd say to some kid on the sidewalk, "where's your Fortuna T-shirt?" Or "Nancy Lou?"—making up names as he went along—"get on over to that school-house! Buy a shirt today, save a school tomorrow!"

Adelsack was so pleased, all she could do was rub her hands together and look gleeful.

When the church let out on nearby Oakcrest, there was such a bottleneck in front of the Wagners' that Dennis's father had to get out in the street to direct traffic. What really surprised me was seeing Coach Reese out there in his Sunday suit and tie helping him. He even had his whistle and was making these polite little *blips* and *bleeps* that we'd never once heard inside the gym.

I was about to decide the ground forces were having all the fun when I heard the unmistakable sound of a helicopter. At first I was mad: *Now I can't hear Eddie broadcasting!*

Then I discovered the chopper was zeroing in on us. I caught my breath, too startled at first to move.

"Grab the tent!" Adelsack yelled, and we dived for it just in time. The nylon rainfly flapped crazily, my T-shirt blew up over my head. I half expected to see Adelsack airborne, skinny as she is, when the helicopter veered sharply off to the right and we saw the printing on the side.

"Newswatch Two!" we both shouted above the noise of the rotors.

Right away Adelsack let loose of the tent and tucked in her T-shirt. I didn't care how I looked, I just started jumping around, screaming, "We did it, we did it!" Fortuna Middle School was being televised! We were newsworthy, after all!

The parking lot started filling fast after that, with kids and dogs and teen-agers and cars. School colors showed up everywhere. People were shouting or pointing. I felt goose bumps rise along my arms.

The next time the chopper made a pass over us, Adelsack and I tried hard to look like serious demonstrators. We held tight to the main tent ropes, hoping we wouldn't get blown away, and smiled at the camera we couldn't quite see. One of our pennants was whipped off that time and fluttered to the ground. Quickly, we reinforced the ones that were left.

The helicopter went off. It appeared to be making a long, wide sweep of the whole area. That's when this bunch of kids came running across the street from the Wagners', all in yellow T-shirts and jeans. Steve was ahead of them hurrying everyone else along.

"Hey, Steve!" I yelled, but he didn't stop.

My stomach lurched when I saw Lisa was right behind him! I pulled out my comb. What was she going to think about me *now*? My goose bumps surrendered to hot flashes and I felt like ducking in the tent. Instead, I stood there glued to the tar and gravel roof, spellbound by what was going on below us.

Steve was shoving everyone around, getting them into some kind of formation. Three of the girls crouched with their heads down, as if playing leapfrog. Karen and Sherry and Greg hugged the ground in the same position, only farther over. From above they looked like blobs of yellow paint dropped in a straight line. Then Steve, Lisa, and (I had to look twice!) my own sister, Delilah, stretched out on their backs to make a long, broken line of yellow-shirted bodies.

Adelsack caught on at once. "It's Morse code, Norman, the international SOS!"

Of course! Eddie's Morse code! Steve was right on target. If anyone needed saving, Fortuna did!

Our combined wills must have brought the helicopter back again, because seconds later there it was, heading toward us once more. Adelsack and I pointed frantically to the distress call, coded with student bodies on the parking lot. Dot, dot, dot, three dashes, three more dots. Yellow on asphalt, it was beautiful!

"They got it!" Adelsack motioned wildly. "I think they got it."

The chopper took a sharp turn, hovered in midair like a dancing mosquito, then rose up for another long pass over the parking lot. They were almost even with us that time. We could actually see the cameraman!

The high point of all that for me was hearing Lisa screeching "You're a hero, Norman Gates!" I'd swear it was her voice. There was a lot of clapping and yelling going on after the SOS got to its feet, but Lisa's words were the ones that reached my ears. Even the music of the six-member band that had just arrived and was playing its brass heart out didn't thrill me as much as Lisa's words: *You're a hero, Norman Gates!* As long as I live, I'll never forget how good that made me feel. Being called a hero can definitely boost the average guy to heights he never dreamed of.

Things almost got out of hand after that. Reporters showed up from another TV station and from the *Valley News*. They were mobbed by students but still managed to take tons of pictures at the school and at the Wagners' place both.

The climax of the whole affair was when Newswatch Two airlifted a reporter onto the roof of the school with half the student body looking on. We weren't expecting that, even though we'd seen the helicopter set down a few minutes earlier on the football field. Bracing the tent again, Adelsack and I watched with our mouths open as the newsman got out of the harness, waved the chopper away, and started toward us, his clothes pasted against his body by the rush of air.

However, Newswatch Two's timing turned out to be the world's worst. The reporter hadn't been there five minutes when the oversize door above the stage opened up and Mr. Clayton himself walked out. My heart sank. Behind him came Mr. Gray, our school board representative, and a law officer who looked tough enough to be the warden at Sing Sing. There they came, marching toward us across the roof like a blooming battalion of Secret Service men.

"Don't flinch, Norman," Adelsack said, down low.

I wasn't flinching. What I was experiencing was a total body spasm!

Immediately, Adelsack took charge of the situation.

"If you gentlemen will wait a minute," she said, looking dead straight into their eyes, "we'll finish talking to this reporter first. He came up the hard way." The newsman grinned. He knew he was getting an exclusive, being right there for the showdown.

So that's exactly what we did. We answered every one of the man's questions before Adelsack was hauled off for (1) disturbing the peace, (2) harassment, and (3) contributing to the delinquency of a minor. Even then, she took time to shake my hand.

When the law officer took Adelsack's arm to lead her away, I felt just like smashing him in the face. If I'd been Steve, I would have!

I guess Mr. Clayton was reading my mind. Next thing I knew, I was being escorted away too, and Mr. Clayton's hand felt very firm on my shoulder.

19

Exiting from the school by way of the catwalks above the stage, I broke into a sweat picturing Adelsack in jail and me in juvenile detention. Almost as bad, I had to hold sweaty hands with Mr. Clayton. I'd hate being roped up with him as my climbing partner. He nearly knocked me off twice before asking if he could hold on to me.

"I'm sorry, Norman," he said, "I have this deathly fear of heights."

The TV man followed us down, asking Mr. Gray questions as we went. Then he took more footage of us as Adelsack got into her car and the deputy put me in his. My skin was crawling like any criminal's would upon capture.

"I believe I'd contact a lawyer if I were you," the officer said to Adelsack before we all drove away. "You're vulnerable to every one of those charges I mentioned earlier."

Although they had me plenty scared, all they did then was "remove us from the premises." In other words, they made us leave. Mom and I were both driven home in this marked county car (Dee preferred to walk) and told to stay away from the school the rest of the day.

We had no intention of going back there. As it turned out, we didn't need to. When it was time for the Sunday night TV news, our house was crammed with people—Pugsleys, Harringtons, the Sweitzers, Dee's friends. It was crazy! I kept wishing my dad was home to join in what turned out to be a real celebration.

The TV coverage that night was phenomenal. Though the reporters tried to present both sides, those great pictures—of Adelsack and me bravely defending our tent, the human SOS laid out on asphalt, and Dennis with his T-shirt concession—were definitely in our favor.

I didn't look half bad on color TV. Even Dee said so . . . though Mom told me my sister was mortified when she first heard *where* and *with whom* I'd spent the night.

Adelsack came off looking passable too, in her blue sweats and yellow T-shirt, though I was still faintly reminded of a grasshopper—the way she jumped around grabbing the tent and everything.

After the news was over, Lisa cornered me.

"How would you like to manage my campaign for class president next fall?" she asked.

"I'm your man."

"Even if you have to commute to Clearfield to do it," she added, treating me to a dimply smile.

"But I thought you wanted to be eighth-grade *secretary*."

"Norman, I just decided to go for it. Think big! Isn't that your motto?"

My chest swelled noticeably when she said that.

Before that crazy Sunday was over, word got around that Dennis Wagner's father had offered his legal services to the PTA committee and Mrs. Adelsack both. What the Fortuna forces needed all along and couldn't afford—a lawyer—they now had for nothing. Things were definitely looking brighter.

For the next two weeks Fortuna's plight became "the talk of the town," to quote my favorite teacher. With letters pouring in to the *Valley News* and follow-ups appearing nightly on the TV, the school board lost all interest in going after one little old teacher and a mere kid. No one ever did press charges against us. The board and the district suddenly had their hands full trying to look good.

In the end, the school board reopened negotiations. They not only decided to share Fortuna's space with a branch library, they also took in a private preschool and allowed Merriweather Novelty to install a vending machine to raise money for reference books. Our school had a future once more! The Fortuna family was still intact!

After that, Mom quit using words like *waffle-brained* to describe the members of the board. She and Mildred Fensley and Mr. Gray got quite chummy before all the leases were signed.

There was so much harmony, in fact, Steve got restless and started a fight. It was with Gary Wannamaker this time, who had the bad judgment to call Mrs. Adelsack a Sweatbag. It took Coach Reese and Mr. Trotter both to break them up.

The high point for Adelsack must have been our final assembly, which was—simply and meaningfully—entitled "Fortuna Forever."

Adelsack had become something of a folk hero those last weeks of school. When word got around about her upcoming promotion to Title IX Supervisor, everybody wanted to do something. Right away the student body officers started circulating a petition.

114

Imagine how hushed the auditorium was when Mr. Clayton presented Mrs. Adelsack with a four-page petition that had been signed by *every* boy and girl in the school.

"The students of Fortuna Middle School are proud to announce"—and there Mr. Clayton stopped to clear his throat—"that the new public library shall hereinafter be called the Geraldine Adelsack Branch."

You should have heard the cheering *then*.

Mrs. Adelsack was so impressed, she cried. She also made Mr. Clayton install the students' signatures (including Wannamaker's) under glass in the trophy case, where they will reside permanently.

The letter I'd wanted all along came the last week of school. Even though it was addressed c/o Barbara Gates, it had my name on it. It started out *Dear Norman.*

Dad apologized first for telephoning when I was at the movies with Steve—as if that was his fault. He said he'd especially wanted to hear my voice. Then he told me what he'd already told Mom, about two of the climbers getting frostbite and the miserable dysentery they all had. I could tell he was disappointed they weren't going on to Nepal, but he also admitted he was terribly homesick. I could understand that. I'd been homesick for him for four whole months!

Brady wants to include us in some climbing this summer, Dad wrote near the end, *said he wouldn't mind a bit if Steve came along, too. I think he envies me, having a son your age.*

There was some personal stuff in the last paragraph that I don't think he'd say face-to-face, but that I plan to keep at the bottom of my Tootsie Roll bank forever.

I guess it was the letter that put my fears to rest at last. I don't know how I'd got things so messed up in my mind, except that I was scared and mad and lonesome all at once. Of course, Mom's always pointing out that I'm an extremely creative worrier. There might be some truth to what she says.

20

At long last we're on our way to the airport to pick up my dad. Mom's wearing the new wraparound skirt she made, I've just had my first permanent, and Dee has on her favorite designer jeans with the label on the back pocket.

We're all pretty excited. I can't wait to see my dad again —new beard and all—and hear about his climbing adventures. I'm glad we have something exciting to tell him, too. It's not as if our lives were exactly dull while he was away!

You might like to know Mom burned the IOU she was holding on me. Dennis Wagner sold all the T-shirts that day except two large ones that Mom glommed on to at the last minute. One we're saving for Dad. The other we sent to Grandpa Middal in a big envelope with newspaper clippings. When he called to thank us, he said he was mighty proud to have the same name as me.

Anyway, today we really look like a family. We're all wearing our yellow Fortuna Forever shirts. All except Animal, that is, who keeps sitting on me here in the backseat of the car. I guess he doesn't know a hero when he sees one. (The thing my dog *did* notice through all the excitement this spring was that my voice was changing. He looks confused when I talk to him, cocking his head to one side, as if the new manly voice and the undersize body don't go together.)

Now, with the perfect summer stretching ahead of us, I've actually persuaded Mom to let up on the vocabulary lessons at home.

"Come on," I'd begged her the night she was trying to get out her grades, "already I'm tenacious and sagacious, besides being voracious. I'll be wise before my time if you keep this up."

"Okay, Normie," she said, laughing at me. (She's been doing a lot of laughing lately.) "You choose the last two words, then we'll hold off until September."

It was a pleasure to be in charge. I got busy with the Magic Marker, and before I knew it my two words were tightly secured under the strawberry magnets.

To tell you the truth, I don't know if they're adjectives or nouns or participles. I don't think it matters. It's the meaning that counts.

"Welcome home!" it says there on our refrigerator door.

Constance Greene

One author who makes kids *laugh at themselves*— when growing up gets them down.

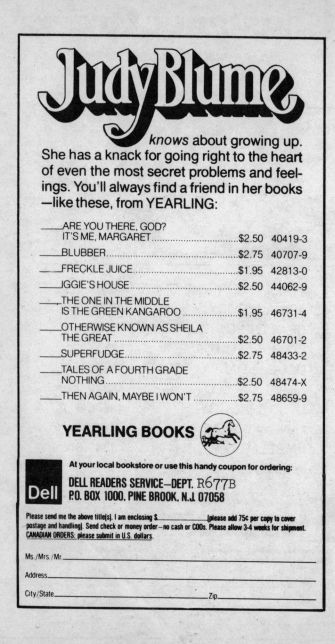